# Like Life

# Like Life

STORIES

*Lorrie Moore*

ALFRED A. KNOPF ⌘ NEW YORK 1990

THIS IS A BORZOI BOOK
PUBLISHED BY ALFRED A. KNOPF, INC.

Most of the stories in this collection were originally published in somewhat different
form in the following publications: GQ: "Two Boys." The New York Times
Book Review: "Starving Again." New York Woman: "Vissi d'Arte." The
New Yorker: "You're Ugly, Too," "The Jewish Hunter." Tampa Review:
"Places to Look for Your Mind."

Grateful acknowledgment is made to the following for permission to reprint previously
published material: CPP/BELWIN, INC., AND INTERNATIONAL MUSIC PUB-
LICATIONS: Excerpt from "Almost Like Being in Love" by Alan Jay Lerner and
Frederick Loewe. Copyright 1947 (Renewed 1975) by Alan Jay Lerner and
Frederick Loewe. World rights assigned to Chappell & Co., Inc. World rights
assigned to and controlled by EMI U Catalog. Open market rights administered
by International Music Publications. International copyright secured. Made in
U.S.A. All rights reserved. Used by permission. E. P. DUTTON: Excerpt from A
Child's History of Art by V. M. Hillyer and E. G. Huey. Copyright 1933
by Appleton-Century Co., Inc. Copyright renewed 1961 by D. Appleton-Century
Co., Inc., and Mercantile Safe Deposit and Trust Co. Reprinted by permission.

Library of Congress Cataloging-in-Publication Data
Moore, Lorrie.
Like life / Lorrie Moore. — 1st ed.
p.   cm.
ISBN 0-394-58101-6
I. Title.
PS3563.06225L5   1990
813'.54—dc20     89-43363   CIP

Manufactured in the United States of America
FIRST EDITION

For making the slow going less slow, the author wishes to thank the Corporation of Yaddo, the University of Wisconsin Graduate School, the Wisconsin Arts Board, the National Endowment for the Arts, and the Rockefeller Foundation.

# Contents

*It seemed very sad to see you going off in your new shoes alone.*
—Zelda Fitzgerald, in a letter to her husband, February 1932

# Like Life

# Two
# Boys

FOR THE FIRST TIME in her life, Mary was seeing two boys at once. It involved extra laundry, an answering machine, and dark solo trips in taxicabs, which, in Cleveland, had to be summoned by phone, but she recommended it in postcards to friends. She bought the ones with photos of the flats, of James Garfield's grave, or an Annunciation from the art museum, one with a peacock-handsome angel holding up fingers and whispering, *One boy, two boys.* On the back she wrote, *You feel so attended to! To think we all thought just one might amuse, let alone fulfill. Unveil thyself! Unblacken those teeth and minds! Get more boys in your life!*

Her nervous collapse was subtle. It took the form of trips to a small neighborhood park, for which she dressed all in white: white blouses, white skirts, white anklets, shoes flat and white as boat sails. She read Bible poetry in the shade on the ground or else a paperback she had found about someone alone on a raft in the ocean, surviving for forty days and nights on nail parings and fish. Mary spoke to no one. She read, and tried not to worry about grass stains, though sometimes she got up and sat on a bench, particularly if there was a clump of something nearby, or a couple making out. She needed to be unsullied, if only for an afternoon. When she returned home, she clutched her books and averted her gaze from the men unloading meat in front of her building. She lived in a small room above a meat company—Alexander Hamilton Pork—and in front, daily, they wheeled in the pale, fatty carcasses, hooked and naked, uncut, unhooved. She tried not to let the refrigerated smell follow her in the door, up the stairs, the vague shame and hamburger death of it, though sometimes it did. Every day she attempted not to step in the blood that ran off the sidewalk and collected in the gutter, dark and alive. At five-thirty she approached her own building in a halting tiptoe and held her breath. The trucks out front pulled away to go home, and the Hamilton Pork butchers, in their red-stained doctors' coats and badges printed from ten-dollar bills, hosed down the sidewalk, leaving the block glistening like a canal. The squeegee kids at the corner would smile at Mary and then, low on water, rush to dip into the puddles and smear their squeegees, watery pink, across the windshields of cars stopped for the light. "Hello," they said. "Hello, hello."

"Where have you been?" asked Boy Number One on the phone in the evening. "I've been trying to reach you." He was running for a local congressional seat, and Mary was working for him. She distributed fliers and put up posters on kiosks and trees. The posters consisted of a huge, handsome photograph with the words *Number One* underneath. She usually tried to staple him through the tie, so that it looked like a clip, but when she felt tired, or when he talked too much about his wife, she stapled him right in the eyes, like a corpse. He claimed to be separating. Mary knew what *separating* meant: The head and the body no longer consult; the wife sleeps late, then goes to a shrink, a palm reader, an acupuncturist; the fat rises to the top. Number One was dismantling his life. Slowly, he said. Kindly. He had already fired his secretary, gotten a new campaign manager, gone from stocks to bonds to cash, and sold some lakefront property. He was liquidating. Soon the sleeping wife. "I just worry about the boys," he said. He had two.

"Where have I been?" echoed Mary. She searched deep in her soul. "I've been at the park, reading."

"I miss you," said Number One. "I wish I could come see you this minute." But he was stuck far away in a house with a lid and holes punched in for air; there was grass at the bottom to eat. He also had a small apartment downtown, where the doorman smiled at Mary and nodded her in. But this evening One was at the house with the boys; they were sensitive and taciturn and both in junior high.

"Hmmm," said Mary. She was getting headaches. She wondered what Number Two was doing. Perhaps he could come over and rub her back, scold the pounding and impounding out of her temples, lay on hands, warm and moist. "How is your wife?" asked Mary. She looked at her alarm clock.

"Sleeping," said One.

"Soon you will join her cold digits," said Mary. One fell silent. "You know, what if I were sleeping with somebody else too?" she added. One plus one. "Wouldn't that be better? Wouldn't that be even?" This was her penchant for algebra. She wasn't vengeful. She didn't want to get even. She wanted to be even already.

"I mean, if I were sleeping with somebody else also, wouldn't that make everyone happy?" She thought again of Boy Number Two, whom too often she denied. When she hung up, she would phone him.

"*Happy?*" hooted Number One. "More than happy. We're talking delirious." He was the funny one. After they made love, he'd sigh, open his eyes, and say, "Was that you?" Number Two was not so hilarious. He was tall and depressed and steady as rain. Ask him, "What if we both saw other people?" and he'd stare out the window, towering and morose. He'd say nothing. Or he'd shrug and say, "Fthatz . . ."

"Excuse me?"

"Fthatz what you want." He'd kiss her, then weep into his

own long arm. Mary worried about his health. Number One always ate at restaurants where the food—the squid, the liver, the carrots—was all described as "young and tender," like a Tony Bennett song. But Number Two went to coffee shops and ate things that had nitrites and dark, lacy crusts around the edges. Such food could enter you old and sticking like a bad dream. When Two ate, he nipped nothing in the bud. It could cause you to grow weary and sad, coming in at the tail end of things like that.

"You have everything," she said to Number One. "You have too much: money, power, women." It was absurd to talk about these things in a place like Cleveland. But then the world was always small, no matter what world it was, and you just had to go ahead and say things about it. "Your life is too crowded."

"It's a bit bottlenecked, I admit."

"You've got a ticket holders' line so long it's attracting mimes and jugglers." At times this was how they spoke.

"It's the portrait painters I'm worried about," said One. "They're aggressive and untalented." A click came over the line. He had another call waiting.

"It's so unfair," said Mary. "Everybody wants to sit next to you on the bus."

"I've got to get off the phone now," he said, for he was afraid of how the conversation might go. It might go and go and go.

IN THE PARK an eleven-year-old girl loped back and forth in front of her. Mary looked up. The girl was skinny, flat-chested, lipsticked. She wore a halter top that left her bare-backed, shoulder blades jutting like wings. She spat once, loud and fierce, and it landed by Mary's feet. "Message from outer space," said the girl, and then she strolled off, out of the park. Mary tried to keep reading, but it was hard after that. She grew distracted and uneasy, and she got up and went home, stepping through the blood water and ignoring the meat men, who, when they had them on, tipped their hair-netted caps. Everything came forward and back again, in a wobbly dance, and when she went upstairs she held on to the railing.

THIS WAS WHY she liked Boy Number Two: He was kind and quiet, like someone she'd known for a long time, like someone she'd sat next to at school. He looked down and told her he loved her, sweated all over her, and left his smell lingering around her room. Number One was not a sweater. He was compact and had no pores at all, the heat building up behind his skin. Nothing of him evaporated. He left no trail or scent, but when you were with him, the heat was there and you had to touch. You got close and lost your mind a little. You let it swim. Out into the middle of the sea on a raft. Nail parings and fish.

When he was over, Number Two liked to drink beer and go to bed early, whimpering into her, feet dangling over the bed. He gave her long back rubs, then collapsed on top of her in a moan. He was full of sounds. Words came few and slow. They were never what he meant, he said. He had a hard time explaining.

"I know," said Mary. She had learned to trust his eyes, the light in them, sapphirine and uxorious, though on occasion something drove through them in a scary flash.

"Kiss me," he would say. And she would close her eyes and kiss.

SOMETIMES in her mind she concocted a third one, Boy Number Three. He was composed of the best features of each. It was Boy Number Three, she realized, she desired. Alone, Number One was rich and mean. Number Two was sighing, repetitive, tall, going on forever; you just wanted him to sit down. It was inevitable that she splice and add. One plus two. Three was clever and true. He was better than everybody. Alone, Numbers One and Two were missing parts, gouged and menacing, roaming dangerously through the emerald parks of Cleveland, shaking hands with voters, or stooped moodily over a chili dog. Number Three always presented himself in her mind after a drink or two, like an escort, bearing gifts and wearing a nice suit. "Ah, Number Three," she would say, with her eyes closed.

"I love you," Mary said to Number One. They were being concubines together in his apartment bedroom, lit by streetlights, rescued from ordinary living.

"You're very special," he replied.

"You're very special, too," said Mary. "Though I suppose you'd be even more special if you were single."

"That would make me more than special," said Number One. "That would make me rare. We're talking unicorn."

"I love you," she said to Number Two. She was romantic that way. Her heart was big and bursting. Though her brain was drying and subdividing like a cauliflower. She called both boys "honey," and it shocked her a little. How many honeys could you have? Perhaps you could open your arms and have so many honeys you achieved a higher spiritual plane, like a shelf in a health food store, or a pine tree, mystically inert, life barking at the bottom like a dog.

"I love you, too," said Two, the hot lunch of him lifting off his skin in a steam, a slight choke in the voice, collared and sputtering.

THE POSTCARDS from her friends said, *Mary, what are you doing!?* Or else they said, *Sounds great to me.* One of them said, *You hog,* and then there were a lot of exclamation points.

She painted her room a resonant white. Hope White, it was called, like the heroine of a nurse novel. She began collecting white furniture, small things, for juveniles, only they were for her. She sat in them and at them and felt the edge of a childhood she'd never quite had or couldn't quite remember float back to her, cleansing and restoring. She bathed in Lysol, capfuls under the running tap. She moved her other furniture—the large red, black, and brown pieces—out onto the sidewalk and watched the city haul them away on Mondays, until her room was spare and milky as a bone.

"You've redecorated," said Number One.

"Do you really love me?" said Number Two. He never looked around. He stepped toward her, slowly, wanting to know only this.

IN THE PARK, after a Lysol bath, she sat on the paint-flaked slats of a bench and read. *Who shall ascend the hill of the Lord?* . . . *He who has clean hands* . . . There was much casting of lots for raiment. In the other book there was a shark that kept circling.

The same eleven-year-old girl, lips waxed a greenish peach, came by to spit on her.

"*What?*" said Mary, aghast.

"Nothin'," said the girl. "I'm not going to hurt you," she mocked, and her shoulders moved around as children's do when they play dress-up, a bad imitation of a movie star. She had a cheap shoulder bag with a long strap, and she hoisted it up over her head and arranged it in a diagonal across her chest.

Mary stood and walked away with what might have been indignation in someone else but in her was a horrified scurry. They could see! Everyone could see what she was, what she was doing! She wasn't fooling a soul. What she needed was plans. At a time like this, plans could save a person. They could organize time and space for a while, like little sculptures. At home Mary made soup and ate it, staring at the radiator. She would plan a trip! She would travel to some place far away, some place unlittered and pure.

She bought guidebooks about Canada: Nova Scotia, New Brunswick, Prince Edward Island. She stayed in her room, away from spitters, alternately flipped and perused the pages of her books, her head filling like a suitcase with the names of hotels and local monuments and exchange rates and historical episodes, a fearful excitement building in her to an exhaustion, travel moving up through her like a blood, until she felt she had already been to Canada, already been traveling there for months, and now had to fall back, alone, on her bed and rest.

MARY WENT to Number One's office to return some of the fliers and to tell him she was going away. It smelled of cigarettes and cigars, a public place, like a train. He closed the door.

"I'm worried about you. You seem distant. And you're always dressed in white. What's going on?"

"I'm saving myself for marriage," she said. "Not yours."

Number One looked at her. He had been about to say "Mine?" but there wasn't enough room for both of them there, like two men on a base. They were arriving at punch lines together these days. They had begun to do imitations of each other, that most violent and satisfying end to love.

"I'm sorry I haven't been in to work," said Mary. "But I've decided I have to go away for a while. I'm going to Canada. You'll be able to return to your other life."

"What other life? The one where I walk the streets at two in the morning dressed as Himmler? That one?" On his desk was a news clipping about a representative from Nebraska who'd been having affairs far away from home. The headline read: RUNNING FOR PUBLIC ORIFICE: WHO SHOULD CAST THE FIRST STONE? The dark at the edge of Mary's vision grew inward, then back out again. She grabbed the arm of a chair and sat down.

"My life is very strange," said Mary.

One looked at her steadily. She looked tired and lost. "You know," he said, "you're not the only woman who has ever been involved with a married—a man with marital entanglements." He usually called their romance a *situation*. Or sometimes, to entertain, *grownuppery*. All the words caused Mary to feel faint.

"Not the only woman?" said Mary. "And here I thought I was blazing new paths." When she was little her mother had said, "Would you jump off a cliff just because everybody else did?"

"Yes," Mary had said.

"*Would* you?" said her mother.

Mary had tried again. "No," she said. There were only two answers. Which could it be?

"Let me take you out to dinner," said Number One.

Mary was staring past him out the window. There were women who leaped through such glass. Just got a running start and did it.

"I have to go to Canada for a while," she murmured.

"Canada." One smiled. "You've always been such an adventuress. Did you get your shots?" This is what happened in love. One of you cried a lot and then both of you grew sarcastic.

She handed him his fliers. He put them in a pile near a rhinoceros paperweight, and he slid his hand down his face like a boy with a squeegee. She stood and kissed his ear, which was a delicate thing, a sea creature with the wind of her kiss trapped inside.

TO BOY NUMBER TWO she said, "I must take a trip."

He held her around the waist, afraid and tight. "Marry me," he said, "or else."

"Else," she said. She always wanted the thing not proposed. The other thing.

"Maybe in two years," she mumbled, trying to step back.

They might buy a car, a house at the edge of the Heights. They would grow overweight and rear sullen and lazy children. Two boys.

And a girl.

Number One would send her postcards with jokes on the back. *You hog.*

She touched Number Two's arm. He was sweet to her, in his way, though his hair split into greasy V's and the strange, occasional panic in him poured worrisomely through the veins of his arms.

"I need a break," said Mary. "I'm going to go to Canada."

He let go of her and went to the window, his knuckles hard little men on the sill.

SHE WENT to Ottawa for two weeks. It was British and empty and there were no sidewalk cafés as it was already October and who knew when the canals might freeze. She went to the National Gallery and stood before the Paul Peels and Tom Thompsons, their Mother Goose names, their naked children and fiery leaves. She took a tour of Parliament, which was richly wooden and crimson velvet and just that month scandalized by the personal lives of several of its members. "So to speak"—the guide winked, and the jaws in the group went slack.

Mary went to a restaurant that had once been a mill, and she smiled at the waiters and stared at the stone walls. At night, alone in her hotel room, she imagined the cool bridal bleach of the sheets healing her, holding her like a shroud, working their white temporarily through her skin and into the thinking blood of her. Every morning at seven someone phoned her from the desk downstairs to wake her up.

"What is there to do today?" Mary inquired.

"You want Montreal, miss. This is Ottawa."

French. She hadn't wanted anything French.

"Breakfast until ten in the Union Jack Room, miss."

She sent postcards to Boy Number One and to Boy Number Two. She wrote on them, *I will be home next Tuesday on the two o'clock bus.* She put Number One's in an envelope and mailed it to his post office box. She took another tour of Parliament, then went to a church and tried to pray for a very long time. "O father who is the father," she began, "who is the father of us all . . ." As a child she had liked to pray and had always improvised. She had closed her eyes tight as stitches and in the midst of all the colors, she was sure she saw God swimming toward her with messages and advice, a large fortune cookie in a beard and a robe, flowing, flowing. Now the chant of it made her dizzy. She opened her eyes. The church was hushed and modern, lit like a library, and full of women on their knees, as if they might never get up.

She slept fitfully on the way home, the bus rumbling beneath her, urging her to dreams and occasionally to wonder, half in and half out of them, whether anyone would be there at the station to greet her. Boy Number Two would probably not be. He was poor and carless and feeling unappreciated. Perhaps One, in a dash from the office, in a characteristically rash gesture, would take a break from campaign considerations and be waiting with flowers. It wasn't entirely a long shot.

Mary struggled off the bus with her bag. She was still groggy from sleep, and this aspect of life, getting on and off things, had always seemed difficult. Someone spoke her name. She looked to one side and heard it again. "Mary." She looked up and up, and there he was: Boy Number Two in a holey sweater and his hair in V's.

"An announcement," called the PA system. "An announcement for all passengers on . . ."

"Hi!" said Mary. The peculiar mix of gratitude and disappointment she always felt with Two settled in her joints like the beginnings of flu. They kissed on the cheek and then on the mouth, at which point he insisted on taking her bag.

They passed through the crowd uneasily, trying to talk but then not trying. The bus station was a piazza of homelessness and danger, everywhere the heartspin of greetings and departures: humid, ambivalent. Someone waved to them: a barelegged woman with green ooze and flies buzzing close. An old man with something white curled in the curl of his ear approached and asked them for a dollar. "For food!" he assured them. "Not drink! Not drink! For food!"

Two pulled a dollar from his pocket. "There you go, my man," he said. It suddenly seemed to Mary that she would have to choose, that even if you didn't know who in the world to love, it was important to choose. You chose love like a belief, a faith, a place, a box for one's heart to knock against like a spook in the house.

Two had no money for a cab but wanted to walk Mary home, one arm clamped around her back and upper arms. They made their way like this across the city. It used to be that Two would put a big, limp fish hand in the middle of her spine, but Mary would manage to escape, stopping and pointing out something—"Look, Halley's Comet! Look, a star!"—so now he clamped her tightly, pressed against his side so that her shoulders curved front and their hips bumped each other.

Mary longed to wriggle away.

At her door she thanked him. "You don't want me to come upstairs with you?" Two asked. "I haven't seen you in so long." He stepped back, away from her.

"I'm so tired," said Mary. "I'm sorry." The Hamilton Pork men stood around, waiting for another delivery and grinning. Two gave her back her suitcase and said, "See ya," a small mat of Dixie cup and gum stuck to one shoe.

Mary went upstairs to listen to the messages on her machine. There was a message from an old school friend, a wrong number, a strange girl's voice saying, "Who are you? What is your name?" and the quick, harried voice of Number One. "I've forgotten when you were coming home. Is it today?" Then another wrong number. "Who are you? What is your name?" Then Number One's voice again: "I guess it's not today, either."

She lay down to rest and didn't unpack her bag. When the phone rang, she leaped up, and the leap knocked her purse and several books off the bed.

"It's you," said Boy Number One.

"Yes," said Mary. She felt a small, short blizzard come to her eyes and then go.

"Mary, what's wrong?"

"Nothing," she said, and tried to swallow. When tenderness ended, there was a lull before the hate, and things could spill out into it. There was always so much to keep back, so much scratching behind the face. You tried to shoo things away, a broomed woman with a porch to protect.

"Did you have a good trip?"

"Fine. I was hoping you might be there to meet me."

"I lost your postcard and forgot what—"

"That's OK. My brother picked me up instead. I see what my life is: I tell my brother when I'm going to be home, and I tell you when I'm going to be home. Who's there to greet me? My brother. We're not even that close, as siblings go."

One sighed. "What happened was your brother and I flipped a coin and he lost. I thought he was a very good sport about it, though." The line fell still. "I didn't know you had a brother," said One.

Mary lay back on her bed, cradled the phone close. "How does the campaign look?" she asked.

"Money's still coming in, and the party's pleased with the radio spots. I've grown weary of it all. Maybe you could help me. What does the word *constituent* mean? They keep talking about constituents." She was supposed to laugh.

"Yes, well, Canada was a vision," said Mary. "All modern and clean and prosperous. At least it looked that way. There's something terribly wrong with Cleveland."

"Cleveland doesn't have the right people in Washington. Canada does." Number One was for the redistribution of wealth. He was for cutting defense spending. He was for the U.S. out of Latin America. He'd been to Hollywood benefits. But he'd never once given a coin to a beggar. Number Two did that.

"Charity that crude dehumanizes," said Number One.

"Get yourself a cola, my man," said Number Two.

"I have to come pick up my paycheck," said Mary.

"Sandy should have it," said One. "I may not be able to see you, Mary. That's partly why I'm calling. I'm terribly busy."

"Fund-raisers?" She wrapped the phone cord around one leg, which she had lifted into the air for exercise.

"That and the boys. My wife says they're suffering a bit, acting out the rottenness in our marriage."

"And here I thought you and she were doing that," said Mary. "Now everybody's getting into the act."

"You don't know what it's like to have two boys," he said. "You just don't know."

MARY STRETCHED OUT on her stomach, alone in bed. A dismantled Number Three, huge, torn raggedly at the seams, terrorized the city. The phone rang endlessly. Mary's machine picked it up. *Hello? Hello?*

"I know you're there. Will you please pick up the phone?"

"I know you're there. Will you please pick up the phone?"

"I know you're there. I know you're there with someone." There was a slight choking sound. Later there were calls where nobody said anything at all.

In the morning he called again, and she answered. "Hello?"

"You slept with someone last night, didn't you?" said Two.

There was a long silence. "I wasn't going to," Mary said finally, "but I kept getting these creepy calls, and I got scared and didn't want to be alone."

"Oh, God," he whispered, a curse or was it love, before the phone crashed, then hummed, the last verse of something long.

IN THE PARK a young woman of about twenty was swirling about, dancing to some tape-recorded arias and Gregorian chants. A small crowd had gathered. Mary watched briefly: This was what happened to you when you were from Youngstown and had been dreamy and unpopular in high school. You grew up and did these sorts of dances.

Mary sat down at a bench some distance away. The little girl who had twice spat on her walked by slowly, appraising. Mary looked up. "Don't spit on me," she said. Her life had come to this: pleading not to be spat on. Was it any better than some flay-limbed dance to boom box Monteverdi? It had its moments.

Not of dignity, exactly, but of something.

"I'm not going to spit on you," sneered the girl.

"Good," said Mary.

The girl sat down at the far end of the bench. Mary kept reading her book but could feel the girl's eyes, a stare scraping along the edge of her, until she finally had to turn and say, "*What?*"

"Just looking," said the girl. "Not spitting."

Mary closed her book. "Are you waiting for someone?"

"Yup," said the girl. "I'm waiting for all my boyfriends to come over and give me a kiss." She closed her eyes and smacked her lips in the air.

"Oh," said Mary, and opened her book again. The sun was beating down on the survivor. Blisters and sores. Poultices of algae paste. The water tight as glass and the wind, blue-faced, holding its breath. How did one get here? How did one's eye-patched, rot-toothed life lead one along so cruelly, like a trick, to the middle of the sea?

AT HOME the phone rang, but Mary let the machine pick it up. It was nobody. The machine clicked and went through its business, rewound. Beneath her the hooks and pulleys across the meat store ceiling rattled and bumped. In a dream the phone rang again and she picked it up. It was somebody she knew only vaguely. A neighbor of Boy Number Two. "I have some bad news," he said in the dream.

IN THE PARK the little girl sat closer, like a small animal—a squirrel, a munk, investigating. She pointed and said, "I live that way; is that the way you live?"

"Don't you have to be in school?" asked Mary. She let her book fall to her lap, but she kept a finger in the page and her dark glasses on.

The girl sighed. "School," she said, and she flubbed her lips in a horse snort. "I told you. I'm waiting for my boyfriends."

"But you're always waiting for them," said Mary. "And they never get here."

"They're unreliable." The girl spat, but away from Mary, more in the direction of the music institute. "They're dead."

Mary stood up, closed her book, started walking. "One in the sky, one in the ground," the girl called, running after Mary. "Hey, do you live this way? I thought so." She followed behind Mary in a kind of traipse, block after block. When they got as far as the Hamilton Pork Company, Mary stopped. She clutched her stomach and turned to look at the girl, who had pulled up alongside her, perspiring slightly. It was way too warm for fall. The girl stared at the meat displayed in the windows, the phallic harangue of sausages, marbled, desiccated, strung up as for a carnival.

"Look!" said the girl, pointing at the sausages. "There they are. All our old boyfriends."

Mary took off her dark glasses. "What grade are you in?" she asked. Could there be a grade for what this girl knew in her bulleted heart? What she knew was the sort of thing that grew in you like a tree, unfurling in your brain, pushing out into your fingers against the nails.

"Grade?" mimicked the girl.

Mary put her glasses back on. "Forget it," she said. Pork blood limned their shoes. Mary held her stomach more tightly; something was fluttering there, the fruit of a worry. She fumbled for her keys.

"All right," said the girl, and she turned and loped away, the bones in her back working hard, colors spinning out, exotic as a bird rarely seen unless believed in, wretchedly, like a moonward thought.

# Vissi
# d'Arte

HARRY LIVED near Times Square, above the sex pavilion that advertised 25 CENT GIRLS. He had lived there for five years and had never gone in, a fact of which he was proud. In the land of perversities he had maintained the perversity of refusal.

"You've never even stepped in? Just once, during the day?" asked his girlfriend, Breckie. "Just to see? I mean, *I* have." Breckie was finishing up her internship at St. Luke's. She was a surgeon and worked with beating and stabbing victims brought into the emergency room. She liked getting her hands on the insides of a thing. It had to do with her childhood.

"Someday when I'm rich," said Harry. "It's not as if it's free."

Harry was a playwright, which made it, he felt, appropriate to live in the theater district. Also, the rent was cheap and he could play his Maria Callas records loud without causing a stir. The neighborhood, after all, was already in a stir. It was a living, permanent stir. He felt he felt relaxed there. He did.

He did.

And if once in a while a small rodent washed up into the toilet or dashed out from under the radiator, Breckie's cat almost always got it.

Harry had started writing plays because he liked them. He

liked the idea of an audience: live guests in front of live per-
formers. It was like company at holidays: all those real-life,
blood-gorged bodies in one room, those bunches of overdressed
grapes; everyone just had to be polite. They had no choice.
That, thought Harry, was civilization. Harry had had a play
produced once as part of a city competition that had named
him one of the three top up-and-coming under-thirty play-
wrights. His picture had appeared with pictures of the other
two in the *New York Times*, all of them wearing the same tie.
The tie had belonged to the photographer, who had made them
all wear it, individually, like a jacket in a restaurant, but besides
that it had been an exuberant event. The play itself was a bleak,
apocalyptic comedy set in the Sheep Meadow at Central Park
in the year 2050. A ranger stood stage left for the four-hour
duration of the play; other characters had love affairs and con-
versations. It was called *For Hours See a Ranger*, and it had run
for five days in a church basement in Murray Hill.

Since that time Harry had been working on what he hoped
would be his masterpiece. The story of his life. *O'Neillian*, he
called it.

"Sounds like *chameleon*," said Breckie. Her work took a lot
out of her.

"It's about the ragtag American family and the lies we all
tell ourselves."

"I know," she said. "I know."

Harry had been writing the play for years. Mostly he worked
at night, tucked in out of the neighborhood's gaud and glare,
letting what he called "the writing fairies" twinkle down from
their night perches to commune with his pen. He was very
secretive about his work. He had never shown Breckie more
than a page of it, and the two or three times he had taken
portions to the photocopier's it had sent him into the flush and
sweat of the shy. It wasn't that he didn't have confidence in it.
It was simply that the material felt so powerful to him, its

arrangement so delicate, that a premature glimpse by the wrong person might curse it forever. He had drawn heavily from his life for this play. He had included the funniest family anecdotes, the most painful details of his adolescence, and the wrenching yet life-affirming death of his great-aunt Flora, Fussbudget Flora, whose dying word had been "Cripes." He had suffered poverty for this play, and would suffer more, he knew, until its completion, living off the frugally spent prize money and the occasional grant he applied for and received. When his cash was low, he had, in the past, done such things as write articles for magazines and newspapers, but he had taken the work too personally and had had too many run-ins with editors. "Don't fuck with my prose," he'd been known to say in a loud voice.

"But, Harry, we need to shorten this to fit in an illustration."

"You're asking me to eat my children so you can fit in some dumb picture?"

"If you don't want a picture, Harry, go publish in the phone book."

"I have to think about this. I have to think about whether or not I can really eat my children this way." But once he had nibbled at the limbs, he found it was not such a far cry to the vital organs, and soon Harry got good at eating his children. When his articles appeared, often there were two pictures.

And so Harry stopped writing journalism. He also turned down offers to write for "the movies, those pieces of crap" and had had to resist continually the persistent efforts of a television producer named Glen Scarp, who had telephoned him every six months for the last four years, since Harry had won the prize— "Hey, Harry, how's it goin', man?"—trying to get him to write for his television series. "TV," Scarp kept saying, "it's a lot like theater. Its roots are in theater." Harry never watched television. He had an old black-and-white set, but the reception was bad because he and Breckie lived too close to the Empire

State Building, the waves shooting out over them and missing the apartment altogether. Once in a while, usually after he got a call from Glen Scarp, Harry would turn the TV on, just to see if things had changed, but it was always a blare of static and police calls from the squad cars that circled the block like birds. "We're going to have to face it," he said to Breckie. "This television is just a large, broken radio with abstract art on the front."

"I can't live like this anymore," said Breckie. "Harry, we've got to make plans. I can't stand the whores, the junkies, the cops, the bums, the porno theaters—you know what's playing at the corner? *Succulent Stewardesses* and *Meat Man*. I'm moving. I'm moving to the Upper West Side. Are you coming with me?"

"Um," said Harry. They had talked once about moving. They had talked once about marriage. They would have children, and Harry would stay home and write and take care of the children during the day. But this had troubled Harry. During the day he liked to go out. He liked to wander down the street to a coffee shop and read the paper, think about his play, order the rice pudding and eat it slowly, his brain aflame with sugar and caffeine, his thoughts heated to a usable caramel. It was a secret life, and it nourished him in a way he couldn't explain. He was most himself in a coffee shop. He imagined having a family and having to say to his children—tiny squalling children in diapers, children with construction paper and pointed scissors, small children with blunt scissors, mewling, puking children with birdhead scissors or scissors with the ears of a dog—"Now, kids, Daddy's going to a coffee shop now. Daddy'll be back in a while."

"Are you coming with me?" repeated Breckie. "I'm talking you get a job, we get an apartment in a building wired for cable, and we have a *real* life. I can wait for you only so long." She had a cat who could wait for anything: food, water, a mouse under a radiator, a twistie from a plastic bag, which, batted under the rug, might come whizzing back out again, any day now, who knew. But not Breckie. Her cat was vigilant as Madame Butterfly, but Breckie had to get on with things.

Harry tried to get angry. "Look," he said. "I'm not a possession. I may not even belong *with* you, but I certainly don't belong *to* you."

"I'm leaving," she said quietly.

"Aw, Breck," said Harry, and he sank down on the bed and put his hands to his face. Breckie could not bear to leave a man with his hands to his face until he had pulled them away. She sat down next to him, held him, and kissed him deeply, until he was asleep, until the morning, when it would be, when it was, possible to leave.

The first few weeks of living alone were difficult, but Harry got used to it in a way. "One year of living alone," said his old friend Dane in a phone call from Seattle, "and you're ruined for life. You'll be spoiled. You'll never go back." Harry worked hard, as he always had, but this time without even the illusion of company. This time there was just the voice of play and playwright in the bombed-away world of his apartment. He started not to mind it, to feel he was suited in some ways to solitude, to the near weightlessness of no one but himself holding things down. He began to prefer talking on the phone to actually getting together with someone, preferred the bodilessness of it, and started to turn down social engagements. He didn't want to actually sit across from someone in a restaurant, look at their face, and eat food. He wanted to turn away, not deal with the face, have the waitress bring them two tin cans and some string so they could just converse, in a faceless dialogue. It would be like writing a play, the cobbling in the night, the great cavity of mind that you filled with voices, like a dark piñata with fruit.

"Tell me something wonderful," he said to Dane. He would lie on his bed, the phone cradled at his cheek, and stare lonesomely at the steeple made by the shadow of the bookcase against the wall. "Tell me that we are going to die dreamfully and loved in our sleep."

"You're always writing one of your plays on the phone," said Dane.

"I said, something wonderful. Say something about springtime."

"It is sloppy and wet. It is a beast from the sea."

"Ah," said Harry.

Downstairs every morning, when he went to get the paper and head for a coffee shop, there was Deli, the hooker, always in his doorway. Her real name was Mirellen, but she had named herself Deli because when she first came to New York from Jackson, she had liked the name Delicatessen, seen it flashing all over in signs above stores, and though she hadn't known what one was, she knew the name was for her.

"Mornin', Harry." She smiled groggily. She had on a black dress, a yellow short-sleeved coat, and white boots. Scabs of translucent gray freckled her arms.

"Mornin', Deli," said Harry.

Deli started to follow him a bit up the block. "Haven't seen your Breck woman around—how things be with you-all?"

"Fine." Harry smiled, but then he had to turn and walk fast down Forty-third Street, for Deli was smart and sly, and in the morning these qualities made him nervous.

It was the following week that the trucks started coming. Eighteen-wheelers. They came, one by one, in the middle of the night, pulled up in front of the 25 Cent Girls pavilion, and idled there. Harry began waking up at four in the morning, in a sweat. The noise was deafening as a factory, and the apartment, even with the windows closed, filled with diesel fumes. He put on his boots, over his bare feet, and threw on his overcoat, a coat over nothing but underwear and skin, and stomped downstairs.

The trucks were always monstrous, with mean bulldog faces, and eyes of glassy plaid. Their bodies stretched the length of the block, and the exhaust that billowed out of the vertical stovepipe at the front was a demonic fog, something from *Macbeth* or *Sherlock Holmes*. Harry didn't like trucks. Some people, he knew, liked them, liked seeing one, thought it was like seeing a moose, something big and wild. But not Harry.

"Hey! Get this heap out of here!" Harry shouted and pounded on the driver's door. "Or at least turn it off!" He looked up into the cabin, but nobody seemed to be there. He pounded again with his fist and then kicked once with his boot. Curtains in the back of the cabin parted, and a man poked his head out. He looked sleepy and annoyed.

"What's the problem, man?" he said, opening the door.

"Turn this thing off!" shouted Harry over the truck's oceanic roar. "Can't you see what's happening with the exhaust here? You're asphyxiating everyone in these apartments!"

"I can't turn this thing off, man," shouted the driver. He was in his underwear—boxer shorts and a neat white vest.

The curtains parted again, and a woman's head emerged. "What's happening, man?"

Harry tried to appeal to the woman. "I'm dying up there. Listen, you've got to move this truck or turn it off."

"I told you buffore," said the man. "I can't turn it off."

"What do you mean, you can't turn it off?"

"I can't turn it off. What am I gonna do, freeze? We're trying to get some sleep in here." He turned and smiled at the woman, who smiled back. She then disappeared behind the curtain.

"I'm trying to get some sleep, too," yelled Harry. "Why don't you just move this thing somewhere else?"

"I can't be moving this thing," said the driver. "If I be moving this thing, you see that guy back there?" He pointed at his rearview mirror, and Harry looked down the street. "I move and that guy be coming to take my spot."

"Just turn this off, then!" shouted Harry.

The driver grew furious. "What are you, some kind of mental retard? I *already* told you. I can't!"

"What do you mean, you can't. That's ridiculous."

"If I turn this mother off, I can't get it started back up again."

Harry stormed back upstairs and phoned the police. "Yeah, right," said Sgt. Dan Lucey of the Eighteenth Precinct. "As if we don't have more urgent things in this neighborhood than truck fumes. What is your name?"

"Harry DeLeo. Look," said Harry. "You think some guy blowing crack in a welfare hotel isn't having one of the few moments of joy in his whole life. *I* am the one—"

"That's a pretty socially responsible thing to say. Look, mister. We'll see what we can do about the trucks, but I can't promise you anything." And then Officer Lucey hung up, as if on a crank call.

There was no way, Harry decided, that he could stay in his apartment. He would die. He would get cancer and die. Of course, all the best people—Christ, Gershwin, Schubert, theater people!—had died in their thirties, but this did not console him. He went back downstairs, outside, in nothing but his overcoat thrown over a pajama top, and a pair of army boots with the laces flapping. He roamed the streets, like the homeless people, like the junkies and hookers with their slow children and quick deals, like the guys down from Harlem with business to transact, like the women with old toasters and knives in their shopping bags, venturing out from Port Authority on those occasions when the weather thawed. With his overcoat and pajama top, he was not in the least scared, because he had become one of them, a street person, rebellion and desperation in his lungs, and they knew this when he passed. They smiled in welcome, but Harry did not smile back. He wandered the streets until he found a newsstand, bought the *Times*, and then drifted some more until he found an all-night coffee shop, where he sat in a booth—a whole big booth, though it was only him!— and spread out his *Times* and circled apartments he could never ever afford. "1500 dollars; EIK." He was shocked. He grew delirious. He made up a joke: how you could cut up the elk for meat during the winter, but in the months before you could never housebreak the thing. "Fifteen hundred dollars for a lousy apartment!" But gradually the numbers grew more and more abstract, and he started circling the ones for eighteen hundred as well.

By March, Harry found himself gassed out of his apartment, roaming the streets, several nights a week. He went to bed full of dread and trepidation, never knowing whether this particular night would be a Truck Night or not. He would phone the landlord's machine and the police and shout things about lymphoma and emphysema and about being a taxpayer, but the police would simply say, "You've called here before, haven't you." He tried sounding like a different neighbor, very polite, a family man, with children, saying, "Please, sir. The trucks are waking the baby."

"Yeah, yeah, yeah," said the police. Harry called the Health Department, the Community Board, the Phil Donahue people. He referred to Officer Lucey as Officer Lucifer and cited cancer statistics from the Science Times. Most of the time people listened and said they would see what they could do.

In the meantime, Harry quit smoking and took vitamins. Once he even called Breckie in the middle of the night at her new apartment on the Upper West Side.

"Is this an awkward time?" he asked.

"To be honest, Harry, yes."

"Oh, my God, really?"

"Look, I don't know how to tell you these things."

"Can you answer yes-or-no questions?"

"All right."

"Shit, I can't think of any." He stopped talking, and the two of them breathed into the phone. "Do you realize," he said at last, "that I have three plantar's warts from walking around barefoot in this apartment?"

"Yes," she said. "I do now."

"A barnacled sole. That's what I am."

"Harry, I can't be writing your plays with you right now."

"Do you recall any trucks hanging out in front of our building, running their engines all night? Did that happen when you were here, when we were living together, when we were together and living here so much in love?"

"Come on, Harry." There was some muffled noise, the seashell sound of hand over mouthpiece, the dim din of a man's voice and hers. Harry hung up. He put on his Maria Callas records, all in a stack on the phonograph spindle, and left the apartment to roam the streets again, to find an open newsstand, a safe coffee shop that didn't put a maraschino cherry on the rice pudding, so that even when you picked it off its mark remained, soaked in, like blood by Walt Disney.

When he trudged back to his apartment, the morning at last all fully lit, falsely wide-eyed and innocent, the trucks were always gone. There was just Deli in the doorway, smiling. "Mornin', Harry," she'd say. "Have a bad dream?"

"You're up early," said Harry. Usually that was what he said.

"Oh, is it daytime already? Well, I'm gonna get myself a real job, a daytime job. Besides, I've been listening to your records from upstairs." Harry stopped jangling his keys for a moment. The Callas arias sailed faintly out through the windowpanes. "Isn't that fag music, Harry? I mean, don't get me wrong. I like fag music. I really like that song that keeps playing about the VCR."

"What are you talking about?" He had his keys out now, pointed and ready to go. But he kept one shoulder turned slightly her way.

"V-C-R-err," sang Deli. "V-C-Dannemora." Deli stopped and laughed. "Dannemora! That girl's in Sing Sing for sure."

"See you," said Harry.

On his answering machine was a message from Glen Scarp. "Hey, Harry, sorry to call you so early, but hey, it's even earlier out here. And wasn't it Ionesco who said something about genius up with the sun? Maybe it was Odets. . . ." *Odets?* thought Harry. "At any rate, I'm flying into New York in a few days, and I thought we might meet for a drink. I'll phone you when I get in."

"No," said Harry out loud. "No. No."

But it was that very morning, after a short, cold rain, just after he'd opened the windows and gotten the apartment aired out, that the bathroom started acting up. The toilet refused to swallow, gurgling if Harry ran the kitchen faucet, and the tub suddenly and terrifyingly filled with water from elsewhere in the building. Somebody else's bath: sudsy water, with rusty swirls. Harry tried flushing the toilet again, and it rose ominously toward the rim. He watched in horror, softly howling the protests—"Ahhhh! UUUaahhh!"—that seemed to help keep the thing from overflowing altogether.

He phoned the landlord, but no one answered. He phoned a plumber he found in the yellow pages, some place advertising *High Velocity Jet Flush* and *Truck Mounted Rodding Machine*. "Are you the super?" asked the plumber.

"There is no super here," said Harry, a confession that left him sad, like an admission that finally there was no God.

"Are you the landlord?"

"No," said Harry. "I'm a tenant."

"We charge two hundred dollars, automatic, if we visit," said the plumber, calmly. Plumbers were always calm. It wasn't just because they were rich. It had something to do with pipes and sticking your hands into them over and over. "Tell your landlord to give us a call."

Harry left another message on his landlord's machine and then went off to a coffee shop. It was called The Cosmic Galaxy and was full of actors and actresses talking wearily about auditions and getting work and how useless *Back Stage* was, though they bought it faithfully and spread it out over the tables anxiously to read. "What I'm trying to put together here," he overheard one actress say, "is a look like Mindy and a sound like Mork." Harry thought with compassion how any one of these people would mutilate themselves to write a TV episode for Glen Scarp, how people are driven to it, for the ten thousand dollars, for the exposure, for the trashy, shameful love of television, whatever it was, and how he had held out for his play, for his beautiful secret play, which he had been mining for years. But it would be worth it, he believed. When he came triumphantly up from the mine, emerged with his work gorgeous and completed, he would be, he knew, feted with an orchestra, greeted big by a huge brass band—trumpeted!—for there were people who knew he was down there, intelligent people, and they were waiting for him.

Of course, you could be down there too long. You could come up for air, all tired and sooty, and find only a man with a harmonica and a tin can, cymbals banging between his knees.

On Tuesday the suds were gone. Harry pulled the drain closed so that nothing else could come rushing up. Then he washed in the kitchen sink, with a rag and some dish detergent, and went off again to The Cosmic Galaxy.

But on Wednesday morning he woke once more to the sharp poison of diesel fumes in the apartment. He walked into his bathroom cautiously and discovered the tub full to the brim with a brackish broth and bits of green floating in it. Scallions. Miso soup with scallions. "What?" He checked the drain, and it was still closed. He left a message on his landlord's machine that went, "Hey, I've got vegetables in my tub," then he trudged out to a different coffee shop, a far one, on the very edge of the neighborhood, practically up by Lincoln Center, and ordered the cheeseburger deluxe, just to treat himself, just to put himself in touch with real life again. When he returned home, Deli was hovering in his doorway. "Mornin', Harry," said Deli.

"Isn't it afternoon?" asked Harry.

"Whatever," said Deli. "You know, Harry, I been thinking. What you need is to spend a little money on a girl who can treat you right." She inched seductively toward him, took his arm with one hand and with the other began rubbing his buttocks through his jeans.

Harry shook her off. "Deli, don't pull this shit on me! How long have I known you? Every morning for five years I've come out of this building and seen you here, said hello. We've been friends. Don't start your hooker shit with me now."

"Fuck you," said Deli. And she walked away, in a sinuous hobble, up to the corner to stand.

Harry went upstairs to his apartment and slowly opened the door to his bathroom. He reached for the switches to the light and fan and turned them on in a single, dramatic flick.

The tub. The miso soup was gone, but in its stead was a dark brown sludge, a foot deep, sulfurous and bubbled. "Oh, my God," said Harry. It was a plague. First suds. Then vegetables. Then darkness. He would get typhus or liver death. There would be frogs.

He left another message on his landlord's machine, then he phoned Breckie and left one on hers: "I have half the Hudson River backed up into my tub. Sea gulls are circling the building. You are a doctor. Does this mean I could get a sad and fatal ailment?" He had Maria Callas singing in the background; he always did now whenever he phoned Breckie and left messages. "Also, I want to know how seriously involved you are with this guy. Because I'm making plans, Breck. I am."

On Thursday, Glen Scarp called and Harry said yes. Yes, yes, yes.

They met that Monday for drinks at the hotel where Scarp was staying. It was on East Fifty-seventh Street and had a long vaulted entrance, dreamy and mirrored, like Versailles, or a wizard's castle. Scarp was waiting for Harry at the end of the corridor, sitting on a velveteen bench. Harry knew it was Scarp by his look of inventory and indifference for everyone who came down the passageway until he got to Harry. Then he looked bemused. Harry proceeded painfully slow, in a worn-shoed lope, toward the bench. Velveteen spread to either side of Scarp, like hips.

"Hello," said Harry.

Scarp was a short man and stood quickly, aggressively, to greet a tall. "Harry? Glen Scarp. Good to meet you at last." He was not that much older than Harry, and took Harry's hand and shook it gingerly between both of his. This was California ginger, Hollywood ginger. This was the limp of flirtation, the lightness of promise. Harry knew this, of course, but knew this only in the way everyone did, which was *knew it sort of.*

Scarp was wearing a diamond broach, a sparkly broccoli on his lapel, and Harry almost said, "Nice pin," but stopped himself. "Well, good to meet you, too," said Harry. "My whole life these days feels conducted on the phone. It's great to finally see the person behind the voice." This was not true, of course, and the lie of it trickled icily down his back.

"Let's have a drink in here, shall we?" Scarp motioned toward the cocktail lounge, which was all ficus trees and chrome and suffused in a bluish light.

"After you," said Harry, which was how he liked to do things.

"Fabulous," said Scarp, who marched confidently in ahead of Harry, so that Harry got to see the back of Scarp's hair: long, sprayed, and waved as a waterfall.

"I want to tell you again first of all how much I admire your work," said Scarp when they were seated and after they had ordered and Scarp had had a chance to push his sleeves up a bit and glance quickly down at his broach, a quick check.

"I admire yours as well," said Harry. In reality he had never seen Scarp's TV series and had actually heard negative things about it. Supposedly it was about young professionals, and there were a lot of blenders and babies. But this, here, now, was not reality. This was reality's back room. It was called dealing. The key, Harry knew, once you got done with the flattery, was to be charming and quick. That is what these people liked: a good, quick story, a snappy line, a confessional anecdote with polish and perhaps a relative in it. Then they would talk money with you. They would talk ten, fifteen thousand an episode, but that was only starters. Sometimes there was more to be had than that. But Harry was after only a single episode. In and out, like a cold bath. That was all he wanted. In and out. A single episode couldn't hurt his soul, not really. His play would have to sit for a while, but when he returned to it, like a soldier home to his wife, he would be a wealthy man. He would move. He would move somewhere with fresh air, somewhere where Breckie lived.

"Thanks," said Scarp. "So what have you been working on lately? You had the under-thirty prize thing—what was that— three years ago?"

"Three? What year is it now?"

"Eighty-eight."

"Eighty-eight," repeated Harry. "Well, the prize thing was actually then four years ago."

"Not under thirty anymore, I'll bet." Scarp smiled, studying Harry's eyes.

"Nope," said Harry, glancing away. "Not for a while."

"So what have you been doing?"

It was like talking to the playwriting police. You needed alibis. "I've been lying in my apartment," said Harry, "eating bonbons and going, 'What year is this?' "

"Right." Scarp laughed inscrutably. He picked up his drink, then put it down again without taking a sip. "As you know, I'm always looking for writers for the show. I've been doing some of the writing myself lately, and I don't mind that. But I thought you and I should get to know each other. I think you have a great handle on contemporary language and the . . . uh . . ."

"Postmodern imagination?" suggested Harry.

"Absolutely."

"Of the young deracinated American?"

"Absolutely," said Scarp.

*Absolutely*. It wasn't even absolutely to Harry, and he was the one who'd said it.

"So just informally, as friends, tell me what you've been up to," said Scarp. "There's no pressure here, no design. We're just getting to know each other."

"Actually I've been working on this play that I feel pretty good about, but it's long and is taking a lot out of me."

"You know, I used to want to write plays. What's this one about, or can't you talk about it?" Scarp started in on his drink, settling back into a listener's sit.

"I'm primitively secret about my work," said Harry.

"I respect that, absolutely," said Scarp. He scowled. "Your family from this country?"

Harry stared at Scarp: His eyes were lockets of distraction. What did it mean? "Yes," said Harry. He had to get Scarp back, get him interested, and so he began telling Scarp, in the most eloquent sentences he could construct, the story of the town his ancestors had founded in the Poconos, and what had become of it recently with radon gas, and the flight to Philly and Pittsburgh. It was a sad, complicated tale, jeweled with bittersweet wisdom, and he was lifting it in its entirety from the central speech of his play.

"That's amazing," said Scarp, apparently impressed, and it gave Harry confidence. He barreled on ahead, with the story of his parents' marriage, his father's alcoholism, his cousin's sex change operation, and a love affair he had once had with one of the Kennedy girls. These were fragile tales he had managed to hone carefully in the writing of his play, and as he spoke with Scarp the voices of his characters entered his mouth and uttered their lines with poignancy and conviction. One had to say words, and these were the words Harry knew best.

"Astonishing," said Scarp. He had ordered another round of drinks, at the end of which Harry was regaling him with the play's climactic scene, the story of Aunt Fussbudget Flora— funny and wrenching and life-affirming in its way.

"The lights went dim, and the moon spilled onto her pillow in pale oblongs. We were all standing there, gathered in a prayer, when she sighed and breathed her very last word on earth: 'Cripes.' "

Scarp howled in laughter. "Miraculous! What a family you have. A fascinating bunch of characters!" Harry grinned and sat back. He liked himself. He liked his life. He liked his play. He didn't feel uneasy or cheaply spent, using his work this way, or if he did, well, he pushed that to one side.

"Harry," said Scarp, as he was signing for the check. "This has been a real pleasure, let me say."

"Yes, it has," said Harry.

"And though I've got to run right now—to have dinner with someone far less engaging, let me tell you—do I have your word that you will consider writing something for me sometime? We don't have to talk specifically now, but promise me you'll give it some thought. I'm making a troth here."

"And it shall set you free," said Harry. "Absolutely."

"I knew I would like you," said Scarp. "I knew we would hit it off. In fact, where do you live? I'll get a cab and drop you off."

"Uh, that's OK," said Harry, smiling. His heart was racing. "I could use the walk."

"If you're sure," said Scarp. "Listen, this was great. Truly great." He shook Harry's hand again, as limply as before. "Fabulous."

THERE IS A WAY of walking in New York, midevening, in the big, blocky East Fifties, that causes the heart to open up and the entire city to rush in and make a small town there. The city stops its painful tantalizing then, its elusiveness and tease suspended, it takes off its clothes and nestles wakefully, generously, next to you. It is there, it is yours, no longer outwitting you. And it is not scary at all, because you love it very much.

"Ah," said Harry. He gave money to the madman who was always singing in front of Carnegie Hall, and not that badly either, but who for some reason was now on the East Side, in front of something called Carnegie Clothes. He dropped coins in the can of the ski-capped woman propped against the Fuller Building, the woman with the pet rabbit and potted plants and the sign saying, I HAVE JUST HAD BRAIN SURGERY, PLEASE HELP ME. "Thank you, dear," she said, glancing up, and Harry thought she looked, startlingly, sexy. "Have a nice day," she said, though it was night.

Harry descended into the subway, his usual lope invigorated to a skip. His play was racing through him: He had known it was good, but now he really knew. Glen Scarp had listened, amazed, and when he had laughed, Harry knew that all his instincts and choices in those lovely moments over the last four years, carefully mining and sculpting the play, had been right.

His words could charm the jaded Hollywood likes of a Glen Scarp; soon those words, some lasting impression of them, might bring him a ten- or even twenty-thousand-dollar television episode to write, and after that he would never have to suffer again. It would just be him and Breckie and his play. A life that was real. They would go out and out and out to eat.

The E train rattled west, then stopped, the lights flickering. Harry looked at the *Be a Stenographer* ad across from him and felt the world was good, that despite the flickering lights, it basically, amazingly, worked. A man pushed into the car at the far end. "Can you help feed me and my hungry kids?" he shouted, holding out a paper cup, and moving slowly down Harry's side of the car. People placed quarters in the cup or else stared psychotically into the reading material on their laps and did not move or turn a page.

Suddenly a man came into the car from the opposite end. "Pay no attention to that man down there," he called to the riders. "I'm the needy one here!" Harry turned to look and saw a shabbily dressed man with a huge sombrero. He had electric Christmas tree lights strung all around the brim and just above it, like some chaotic hatband. He flicked a button and lit them up so that they flashed around his head, red, green, yellow. The train was still stopped, and the flickering overheads had died altogether, along with the sound of the engine. There was only the dull hum of the ventilating system and the light show from the sombrero. "*I* am the needy one here," he reiterated in the strangely warm dark. "My name is Lothar, and I have come from Venus to arrest Ronald Reagan. He is an intergalactic criminal and needs to be taken back to my planet and made to stand trial. I have come here to see that that is done, but my spaceship has broken down. I need your assistance so that I can get it done."

"Amen!" someone called out.

"Yahoo," shouted Harry.

"Can you help me, people, earthlings. I implore you. Anything you can spare will aid me in my goal." The Christmas tree lights zipped around his head, people started to applaud, and everyone dug into their wallets to give money. When the lights came on, and the train started to go again, even the man with the hungry kids was smiling reluctantly, though he did say to Lothar, "Man, I thought this was *my* car." When the train pulled into Forty-second Street, people got off humming, slapping high fives, low fives, though the station smelled of piss.

Harry's happiness lasted five days, Monday through Friday, like a job. On Saturday he awoke in a funk. The phone had not rung. The mail had brought him no letters. The apartment smelled faintly of truck and sewage. He went out to breakfast and ordered the rice pudding, but it came with a cherry.

"What is this?" he asked the waiter. "You didn't use to do this."

"Maraschino eyeballs." The waiter smiled. "We just started putting them on. You wanna whipped cream, too?"

When he went back home, not Deli but a homeless woman in a cloth coat and sneakers was sitting in his doorway. He reached into his pocket to give her some change, but she looked away.

"Excuse me," he said. "I just have to get by here." He took out his keys.

The woman stood up angrily, grabbing her shopping bags. "No, really, you can sit here," said Harry. "I just need to get by you to get in."

"Thanks a lot!" shouted the woman. Her teeth were gray in the grain, like old wood. "Thanks!"

"Come back!" he called. "It's perfectly OK!" But the woman staggered halfway down the block, turned, and started scream-

ing at him. "Thanks for all you've done for me! I really appreciate
it! I really appreciate everything you've done for me my whole
life!"

To relax, he enrolled in a yoga class. It was held three blocks
away, and the teacher, short, overweight, and knowledgeable,
kept coming over to Harry to tell him he was doing things
wrong.

"Stomach in! Shoulders down! Head back!" she bellowed in
the darkness of the yoga room. People looked. She was not fond
of tall, thin men who thought they knew what they were doing.
"Head back!" she said again, and this time tugged on his hair,
to get his head at the right angle.

"I can't believe you pulled my hair," said Harry.

"Pardon me?" said the instructor. She pressed her knee into
the middle disks of his spine.

"I would just do better," said Harry loudly, "if you wouldn't
keep touching me!"

"All right, all right," said the teacher. "I won't touch you,"
and she walked to the other side of the darkened room, to attend
to someone else. Harry lay back for the deep breathing, spine
pressed against the tough thread of the carpet. He put his hand
over his eyes and stayed like that, while the rest of the class
continued with headstands and cat stretches.

The next week Harry decided to try a calisthenics class
instead. It was across the street from the yoga class and was full
of white people in pastel Spandex. Serious acid disco blared
from the corner speakers. The instructor was a thin black man,
who smiled happily at the class and led them in exercises that
resembled the motion of field hands picking cotton. "Pick that
cotton!" he shouted gleefully, overseeing the group, walking
archly among them. "Pick it fast!" He giggled, clasping his
hands. "Oh, what sweet revenge!" The class lasted an hour and
a half, and Harry stayed on for the next class as well, another
hour and a half. It strangely encouraged and calmed him, and

when he went to the grocery store afterward, he felt almost serene. He lingered at the yogurt and the freshly made pasta. He filled his cart with mineral water, feeling healthy and whole again, when a man one aisle away was caught shoplifting a can of bean-with-bacon soup.

"Hey!" shouted the store manager, and two large shelf clerks grabbed the man with the soup. "I didn't do nothing!" yelled the man with the soup, but they dragged him by the ears across the store floor to the meat counter and the back room, where the butchers worked in the day. There they began to beat him, until he could no longer call out. Trails of red smeared the floor of the canned goods aisle, where his ears had split open like fruit and bled.

"Stop it!" cried Harry, following the men to the swinging meat doors. "There's no reason for this sort of violence!" and after two minutes, the employees finally let the shoplifter go. They shoved him, swollen and in shock, out the swinging doors toward the exit.

Harry turned to several other customers, who, also distressed, had come up behind him. "My God," said Harry. "I had two exercise classes today, and it still wasn't enough." He left his shopping cart and fled the store for the phone booth outside, where he dialed the police. "I would like to report a crime. My name is Harry DeLeo, and I am standing on the corner of Eighth and—"

"Yeah. Harry DeLeo. Trucks. Look, Harry DeLeo, we got real things," and the policeman hung up.

AT NIGHT Harry slept in the other room, the "living" room, the room decorated in what Breckie called Early American Mental Institution, the room away from the windows and the trucks, on the sharp-armed sofa, damp towels pressed at the bottom of the bedroom door, so he would not die in his sleep, though that had always been his wish but just not now. He also pressed towels against the bathroom door, in case of an overflow. Safe, barricaded, sulfurous, sandwiched in damp towels like the deviled eggs his mother used to bring to picnics: When he slept he did so dreamlessly, like a bug. In the mornings he woke early and went out and claimed a booth in The Cosmic Galaxy until noon. He read the *Times* and now even the *Post* and the *News*. Sometimes he took notes in the margins for his play. *He felt shackled in nightmare, and in that constant state of daydream that nightmare gives conception to, creature within creature.* In the afternoons he went to see teen movies starring teens. For brief moments they consoled him in a way he couldn't explain. Perhaps it was that the actors were all so attractive and in high school and lived in lovely houses in California. He had never been to California, and only once in the last ten years—when he had gone home with Breck to visit her parents in Minnesota—had he been in a lovely house. The movies reminded him of Breckie, probably that was it, those poreless faces and hairless arms, those idealistic hearts knowing corruption for the first time and learning it well. Harry would leave the movie theater feeling miserable, stepping out into the daylight like a criminal, shoulders bent into coat-hanger angles, in his body the sick heat of hangover, his jacket rumpled as a sheet.

"Harry, you look like shit," said Deli in front of his building. She was passing out fliers for the 25 Cent Girls pavilion. She was wearing a patched vinyl jacket, a red dress, and black pumps with no stockings. "But hey. Nothing I can do for you—except here." She handed him a flier. *Twenty-five Cents! Cheap, Live, and Naked!* "I got myself a day job—ain't you proud of me, Harry?"

Harry *did* feel proud of her, though it surprised him. It did not feel quite appropriate to feel proud. "Deli, I think that's great," he said anyway. "I really do!" Peep show fliers were a start. Surely they were a start.

"Yeah," said Deli, smiling haughtily. "Soon you be asking me to marry you."

"Yup," said Harry, jiggling the key in the lock. Someone in the middle of the night had been jabbing at it with a knife, and the lock was scraped and bent.

"Hey, put on some of that music again, would you?" But Harry had gotten the door open, and it slammed behind him without his answering.

There was mail: a form letter from an agency interested in seeing scripts; an electric bill; a letter from the Health Department verifying his complaint call and advising him to keep after the precinct dispatcher; a postcard for Breckie from some old friend named Lisa, traveling through Italy. *What a place, gal*, it said. *Hello to Harry.* He put it on his refrigerator with a magnet. He went to his desk and from there stared over at it, then stared back at his desk. He went to the window overlooking the street. Deli was still down there, passing out fliers, but people were not taking them anymore. They were brushing by, pretending not to see, and finally she just stood there, in the middle of the sidewalk, frowning, no longer trying, not thrusting a flier out to anyone, just letting the crowds break in front of her, like a wave, until she turned and walked with them, up to the corner, to the light, and threw her fliers into the trash, the way everyone else had done.

The next day Harry got a phone call from Glen Scarp. "Harry, my man, I'm in Jersey directing a scene for a friend. I've got an hour between seven and eight to have a quick drink with you. I'm taking a chopper. Can you make it?"

"I don't know," said Harry. "I'm busy." It was important to be cagey with these guys, to be a little unavailable, to act as if you, too, had a helicopter. "Can you give me a call back later?"

"Sure, sure," said Scarp, as if he understood too clearly. "How about four-thirty. I'll give you a call then."

"Fine," said Harry. "I should know better then what my schedule's like"—he stifled a cough—"for the evening."

"Exactly," said Scarp. "Fabulous."

Harry kept his dirty clothes in a laundry bag at the bottom of his closet. He grabbed the bag up, crammed into it two other pairs of underwear, which had been floating around, and dashed across the street to the Korean laundromat with a large box of generic heavy-duty laundry detergent. He did his wash in an excited fashion, got pushy in claiming a dryer, went next door and ordered a fried egg sandwich to go, with ketchup, and ate it back at the laundromat, sitting on the window ledge, next to a pimp with a satin tie.

At four-thirty, when Scarp called, Harry said, "All's squared away. Just name the place."

This time they met at a restaurant called Zelda. Harry was wearing clean underwear and socks.

"No one ever uses apostrophes anymore, have you noticed?" said Harry. He had been here before and had, in fact, said this before. "It makes restaurants sound like hurricanes." Zelda specialized in eclectic Louisiana cooking. It served things like salmon fillets with macaroni and cheese, both with bones. Capes, ponchos, and little sundresses hung from the ceiling. It was strictly a crazed southern woman's idea of a restaurant.

Harry and Scarp sat in the bar section, near the piano, hemmed in on every side by potted plants.

Scarp was fishing for descriptions. "There's no—"

"Business like show business!" burst out Harry.

"Yes," said Scarp, a little taken aback. He was dressed in jeans and a linen shirt. Again he wore a broach, this time of peridot and garnet, fastened close to the collar. He was drinking a martini.

Harry wasn't drinking. He'd ordered seltzer water and took big handfuls of mixed nuts from the bowl in front of him. He hadn't had a cigarette since the trucks had started coming, and now he found himself needing something to put in his mouth, something to engage his hand on its journey up from the table and back down again. "So tell me about this thing you were shooting in New Jersey," Harry began amiably, but a nut skin got caught in his throat and he began to choke, his face red and crumpling, frightening as a morel. Scarp pushed the seltzer water toward Harry, then politely looked away.

"It's a project that belongs to an old buddy of mine," said Scarp. Harry nodded at him, but his eyes were tearing and he was gulping down seltzer. Scarp continued, pretending not to notice, pretending to have to collect his thoughts by studying objects elsewhere. "He's doing this film about bourgeois guilt— you know, how you can be bourgeois and an artist at the same time . . ."

"Really," croaked Harry. Water filmed his eyes.

". . . but how the guilt can harrow you and how in the end you can't let it. As Flaubert said, Be bourgeois in your life so that you may be daring in your art."

Harry cleared his throat and started to cough again. The nut skin was still down there, scratching and dry. "I don't trust translations," he rasped. He took an especially large swallow of seltzer and could feel the blood leave his face a bit. There was some silence, and then Harry added, "Did Flaubert ever write a play?"

"Don't know," said Scarp. "At any rate, I was just shooting this one scene for my friend, since he was called away by a studio head. It was a very straightforward cute meet at a pedicurist's. Have you ever had a pedicure?"

"No," said Harry.

" really have to. It's one of the great pleasures of

*plantar's warts. You have to put acid on them,*

"Do you feel all right?" asked Scarp, looking suddenly concerned.

"Fine. It's just I quit smoking. Suddenly there's all this air in my lungs. What's a cute meat?"

"Cute meet? It's Hollywood for where two lovers meet and fall in love."

"Oh," said Harry. "I think I liked myself better before I knew that."

Scarp laughed. "You writers," he said, downing his martini. "*We* writers, I should say. By the way, I have to tell you: I've ripped you off mercilessly." Scarp smiled proudly.

"Oh?" said Harry. Something lined up in him, got in order. His back straightened and his feet unhooked from the table legs.

"You know, when we met last time, I was working on an episode for the show where Elsie and John, the two principals, have to confront all sorts of family issues, including the death of an elderly relative."

"That doesn't really sound like ripping me off."

"Well, what I've done is use some of that stuff you told me about your family and the radon gas—well, you'll see—and that fabulous bit about your Aunt Flora dying while you were dating the Kennedy girl. It's due to air early next month. In fact, I'll give you a call when I find out exactly."

Harry didn't know what to say. The room revolved dizzyingly away from him, dumped him and spun, because he'd never really been part of it to begin with. "Excuse me?" he stammered. His hand started to tremble, and he moved it quickly through his hair.

"I'll give you a call. When it's on." Scarp frowned.

Harry gazed at the striated grain of the table—a to show its innards. "*What?*" he said, finally, sl
He picked up his seltzer, knocked it back f

down with a loud crack. "You'd do that for me? You'd really, honestly, do that for me?" He was starting to yell. The people at the table nearest the piano turned to look. "I have to go."

Scarp looked anxiously at his watch. "Yes, I've gotta run myself."

"No, you don't understand!" said Harry loudly. He stood up, huge over the table. "*I* have to go." He pushed back his chair, and it fell all the way over into a plant. He strode quickly toward the door and pushed against it hard.

The night was just beginning to come, and come warmly, the air in a sweet, garbagey thaw. Midtown was crawling with sailors. They were all youthful and ashore and excited to be this way, in their black and white-trimmed suits, exploring Manhattan and knowing it, in this particular guise, to be a movie set they had bought tickets to, knowing the park was up, *the park is up!* knowing there were girls, and places where there were girls, who would pull you against them, who knew what you knew though they seemed too bonelessly small to. Harry loped by the sailors, their boyish, boisterous clusters, then broke into a run. Old men were selling carnations on the corner, and they murmured indecipherably as he passed. The Hercules was showing *Dirty Desiree* and *Throbbin' Hood*, and sailors were going in. Off-duty taxis sped from their last fares at the theaters to the Burger King on Ninth for something to eat. Putting block after block beneath his feet would clear his heart, Harry hoped, but the sailors: There was no shaking them. They were everywhere, hatless and landlubbed with eagernesses. Up ahead on his block, he saw a woman who looked like Deli strolling off with two of them, one on each arm. And then—it *was* Deli.

He stopped, frozen midstride, then started to walk again. "Aw, Deli," he whispered. But who was he to whisper? He had tried to be a hooker himself, had got on the old hip boots and walked, only to discover he was just—a slut.

*The Battery's down*, he thought. *The Battery's down*. He stood in front of the 25 Cent Girls pavilion. Golden lights winked and dashed around the marquee.

"Wanna buy, man?" hissed a guy urinating at the curb. "I got bitches, I got rods, I got crack."

Harry stepped toward the cashier in the entrance booth. He slid a dollar under the glass, and the cashier slid him back four tokens. "What do I do?" he said, looking at the tokens, but the cashier didn't hear him. Two sailors came up behind, bought four dollars' worth, and went inside, smiling.

Harry followed. The interior was lit and staircased like a discotheque, and all along the outer walls were booths with wooden doors. He passed three of them and then stumbled into the fourth. He closed the door, sat down on the bench, and, taking a deep breath, he wept, hopelessly, for Breckie and for God and for that life here that seemed always parallel to his own, never intersecting, like some opposite shore of river he could never swim across, although he kept trying. He looked at the tokens in his hand. They were leaving bluish streaks in the dampness there, melting if not used. He fumbled, placed one in the slot, and a dark screen lifted from behind the glass. Before him, lit and dancing, appeared a 25 Cent Girl, naked, thirtyish, auburn-haired and pale: *National Geographic* goes to Ireland. There was music playing, and she gyrated to it, sleepy and indifferent. But as he watched she seemed to lift her eyes, to spot him, to head toward his window, slow and smiling, until she was pressing her breast against his pane, his alone. He moaned, placed his mouth against the cold single rose of her nipple, against the hard smeared glass, though given time, in this, this wonderful town, he felt, it might warm beneath his labors, truly, like something real.

# Joy

IT WAS A FALL, Jane knew, when little things were being taken away. Fish washed ashore, and no one ate a clam to save their lives. Oystermen netted in the ocean beds, and the oysters were brought up dead. Black as rot and no one knew why. People far from either coast shuddered to think, saw the seas and then the whole planet rise in an angry, inky wave of chowder the size of a bowl. It was as far as their imaginations would allow, and it was too far. Did this have to do with them? They flicked off their radios, left dishes in the sink, and went out. Or they tuned to a station with songs. It was a season for losing anything small, living trinkets you'd thought were yours—a bracelet of mother-of-pearl, a lover's gift, unhinged and slipping off into the night like something yearning and tired. The rain stopped dry. The ground crumbled to lumps, and animals maddened a little with thirst. Squirrels, smelling water on the road, gnawed through the hoses in cars and later died on the shoulders. "Like so many heads," said a radio announcer, who then played a song.

Jane's cat itself had fleas, just the barest hint, and she was going to get rid of them, take the cat to the groomer's for the bath–dip–comb-out. There were rumors about fleas. They could feast on you five or six times a day and never let go. You could wake up in a night sweat with a rash and your saliva gluey and white, in ligaments as you tried to speak. You could look out at your life and no longer recognize it.

The groomer was at a vet's on the west side of town. It was where rich people took their cats, and it made Jane feel she was giving her cat the best possible care. This was a cat who slept on the pillow next to her at night. This was a cat who came running—happy to see her!—when she drove up in front of the house.

This particular morning she had to bring her cat in before eight. The dogs came in at eight-o-five, and the vet liked the cats to get there earlier, so there would be no commotion. Jane's cat actually liked dogs, was curious about them, didn't mind at all observing them from the safety of someone's arms. So Jane didn't worry too much about the eight o'clock rule, and if she got there late, because of traffic or a delayed start on the coffee she needed two cups of simply to get dressed in the morning, no one seemed to mind. They only commented on how well-behaved her cat was.

It usually took fifteen minutes to get to the west side, such was the sprawl of the town, and Jane played the radio loudly and sang along: "I've forgotten more than she'll ever know about you." At red lights she turned to reassure the cat, who lay chagrined and shedding in the passenger's seat. Ahead of them a station wagon moved slowly, and Jane noticed in the back of it a little girl waving and making faces out the rear window. Jane waved and made faces back, sticking out her tongue when the little girl did, pulling strands of hair into her face, and winking dramatically first on one side and then the other. After several blocks, Jane noticed, however, that the little girl was not really looking at *her* but just generally at the traffic. Jane re-collected her face, pulled in her tongue, straightened her hair. But the girl's father, at the wheel, had already spied Jane in his rearview mirror, and was staring, appalled. He slowed down to get a closer look, then picked up speed to get away.

Jane got in the other lane and switched stations on the radio, found a song she liked, something wistful but with a beat. She loved to sing. At home she had the speakers hooked up in the kitchen and would stand at the sink with a hollow-handled sponge filled with dish detergent and sing and wash, sing and rinse. She sang "If the Phone Don't Ring, I Know It's You" and "What Love Is to a Dove." She blasted her way through "Jump Start My Heart," humming on the verses she didn't know. She liked all kinds of music. When she was a teenager she had believed that what the Muzak station played on the radio was "classical music," and to this day her tastes were generous and unjudging—she just liked to get into the song. Most of the time she tried not to worry about whether people might hear her, though an embarrassing thing had happened recently when her landlord had walked into the house, thinking she wasn't home, and caught her sing-speaking in an English accent. "Excuse me," said the landlord. "I'm sorry."

"Oh," she said in reply. "I was just practicing for the— Are you here to check the fuse box?"

"Yes," said the landlord, wondering who it was these days he was renting his houses out to.

Jane had once, briefly, lived in western Oregon but had returned to the Midwest when she and her boyfriend out there had broken up. He was a German man who made rocking horses and jungle gyms and who had been, like her, new to the community. His English was at times halting and full of misheard vernacular, things like "get town" and "to each a zone." One time, when she'd gotten all dressed up to go to dinner, he told her she looked "hunky-dorky." He liked to live dangerously, always driving around town with his gas tank on E. "Pick a lane and do stay in it," he yelled at other drivers. He made the worst coffee Jane had ever tasted, muddy and burned, but she drank it, and stayed long hours in his bed on Sundays. But after a while he took to going out without her, not coming home until two a.m. She started calling him late at night, letting the phone ring, then driving around town looking for his car, which she usually found in front of a tavern somewhere. It had not been like her to do things like this, but knowing that the town was small enough for her to do it, she had found it hard to resist. Once she had gotten into the car and started it up, it was as if she had crashed through a wall, gone from one room with rules into another room with no rules. When she found his car, she would go into the tavern, and if she discovered him at the bar with his arm flung loosely around some other woman, she would tap him on the shoulder and say, "Who's the go-go girl?" Then she'd pour beer onto his legs. She was no longer herself. She had become someone else, a wild West woman, bursting into saloons, the swinging doors flipping behind her. Soon, she thought, bartenders might fear her. Soon they might shout out warnings, like sailors facing a storm: *Here she comes!* And so, after a while, she left Oregon and came back here alone. She rented a house, got a job first at Karen's Stout Shoppe, which sold dresses to overweight women, then later at the cheese store in the Marshall Field's mall.

For a short time she mourned him, believing he had anchored her, had kept her from floating off into No Man's Land, that land of midnight cries and pets with too many little toys, but now she rarely thought of him. She knew there were only small joys in life—the big ones were too complicated to be joys when you got all through—and once you realized that, it took a lot of the pressure off. You could put the pressure aside, like a child's game, its box ripped to flaps at the corners. You could stick it in some old closet and forget about it.

Jane pulled into the vet's parking lot at ten after eight. She lifted the cat up into her arms, pushed the car door shut with one hip, and went inside. Although the air of the place was slightly sour—humid with animal fear, tense with medicine, muffled howls drifting in from the back—the waiting room felt pleasant to her. Hopeful with ficus trees. There were news-magazines on the tables, and ashtrays made from Italian glass. There were matted watercolors on the wall and a silk-screened sign in a white metal frame saying, ANIMALS MUST BE LEASHED OR HELD. Jane walked up to the large semicircular counter ahead of her and placed the cat down on it. Behind her was a man seated with a leashed and lethargic golden Labrador, and Jane's cat peered around back at it, shivering a little. On the other side of the waiting room was a large poodle with the fierce look of a Doberman. His ears were long and floppy, uncut, and his owner, a young woman in her twenties, kept saying, "Come here, Rex. Lie down, baby."

"Can I help you?" asked the woman behind the counter. She had been staring at a computer screen, tapping at a keyboard and bringing up fiery columns of numbers and dates.

"I'm here to bring my cat in for grooming," said Jane. "My last name is Konwicki."

The woman behind the counter smiled and nodded. She tapped something into the computer. "And the cat's name?" she asked.

"Fluffers," said Jane. She had once thought she would name the cat Joseph, but then she had changed her mind.

The woman rolled her chair away from the computer screen. She picked up a large silver microphone and spoke into it. "Fluffers Konwicki here to be groomed." She set the microphone back down. "The groomer will be out in a minute," she said to Jane. "You can wait over there."

Jane pulled the cat to her chest and went and sat in a fake leather director's chair opposite Rex the poodle. A woman and her two children came in through the front entrance wheeling a baby carriage. The woman held open the door and the little boy and girl pushed the carriage through, all the while peering in and squeaking concerned inquiries and affectionate names. "Gooby, are you OK?" asked the boy. "Gooby knows he's at the doctor's, Mom."

"You kids wait right here," said the mom, and she approached the counter with a weary smile. She brushed her bangs off her head, then placed her hands flat out on the countertop and stared at them momentarily, as if this had been the first opportunity all morning to observe them empty. "We're bringing a cat in for surgery," she said, looking back up. "The name is Miller."

"Miller," said the woman behind the counter. She tapped something into the computer. She shook her head, then got up and looked at a clipboard near the cash register. "Miller, Miller, Miller," she said absently. "Miller. All righty! Here we are!" She smiled at Mrs. Miller. The world was again the well-oiled machine she counted on it to be: All things could eventually be found in it. "You want to wheel the cat back around here?"

Mrs. Miller turned toward her children. "Kids? Wanna bring the kitty back around here?" The little boy and girl pushed the baby carriage forward, their steps solemn and processional. The woman behind the counter stepped out from her usual post and held the door to the back part, the examination room, open. "Wheel the cat right in there," she said. She wore white shoes. You could see that now.

They were all in there for no more than a minute before they returned, the children dragging the empty baby carriage behind them and Mrs. Miller sighing and smiling and thanking the woman in the white shoes, who told her to call sometime after three this afternoon. The anesthesia would be worn off by then, and the doctor would know better what to tell them.

"Thanks again," said Mrs. Miller. "Kids?"

"Mom, look," said the little girl. She had wandered over to where Jane was sitting and had begun to pet Jane's cat, occasionally looking up for permission to continue. "Mom, see—this lady has a cat, too." She called to her mother, but it was her brother who came up and stood beside her. The two of them stuck their tiny, star-like hands deep into the cat's fur and squished them around there.

"You like that?" said Jane to her cat, and the cat looked up at her as if he really couldn't decide. She made Fluffers' head nod a bit, as if he were answering the question.

"What is his name?" asked the little girl. Her hand had found the scruff of the cat's neck and was kneading it. The cat stretched his throat up in enjoyment.

"Fluffers," said Jane.

The girl's voice went up an octave into cat range. "Hi, Fluffers," she half sang, half squeaked. "How are you feeling today, Fluffers?"

"Is he sick?" asked the boy.

"Oh, no," said Jane. "He just comes here for a special kind of bath."

"You getting a bath, Fluffers?" cooed the girl, looking directly into the cat's eyes.

"Our cat is having an operation," said the boy.

"That's too bad," said Jane.

The boy looked at her crossly. "No, it's not," he said. "It's a good thing. Then he'll be all better."

"Well, yes, that's true," said Jane.

"Fluffers licked my finger," said the girl.

Their mother now appeared behind them, placing a palm on each of their heads. "Time to go, kiddos," she said. "Beautiful cat," she said to Jane.

THE CHEESE SHOP Jane worked at, in the new mall outside of town, was called Swedish Isle, and she had recently been promoted to assistant manager. There were always just two of them in the shop, Jane and an older woman named Heffie, who minded the register while Jane stood out in front with the cheese samples, usually spreads and dips placed in small amounts on crackers. Once the manager had come by and told her that Heffie should be doing the samples and Jane should be minding the register and doing the price sheets, but the store manager was also the assistant district manager for the chain and was too busy to come by all that often. So most of the time Jane simply continued doing the samples herself. She liked the customer contact. "Care to try our chive-dill today?" she would ask brightly. She felt like Molly Malone, only friendlier and no cockles or mussels; no real seafood for miles. This was the deep Midwest. Meat sections in the grocery stores read: BEEF, PORK, and FISH STICKS.

"Free?" people would ask and pick up a cracker or a bread square from her plastic tray.

"Sure is." She would smile and watch their faces as they chewed. If it was a man she thought was handsome, she'd say, "No. A million dollars," and then giggle in the smallest, happiest way. Sometimes the beggars—lost old hippies and mall musicians—would come in and line up, and she would feed them all, like Dorothy Day in a soup kitchen. She had read a magazine article once about Dorothy Day.

"A little late, aren't you?" said Heffie today. She was tugging at the front strap of her bra and appeared generally disgruntled. Her hair was thinning at the front, and she had it clipped to the top with barrettes she was too old for. "Had to open up the register myself. It'd be curtains if the manager'd come by. Lucky I had keys."

"I'm sorry," said Jane. "I had to take my cat into the vet's this morning, way over on the west side. Any customers?" Jane gave Heffie an anxious look. It said "Please forgive me." It also said "What is your problem?" and *Have a nice day.* Pleasantness was the machismo of the Midwest. There was something athletic about it. You flexed your face into a smile and let it hover there like the dare of a cat.

"No, no customers," said Heffie, "but you never can tell."

"Well, thanks for opening up," said Jane.

Heffie shrugged. "You doing the samples today?"

"Thought I would, yes," said Jane, flipping through some papers attached to a clipboard. "Unless *you* wanted to." She said this with just a hint of good-natured accusation and good-natured insincerity. Heffie wasn't that interested in doing the samples, and Jane was glad. It was just that Heffie didn't much like doing anything, and whatever Jane did apparently seemed to Heffie like more fun, and easier, so sometimes the older woman complained a little by means of a shrug or a sigh.

"Nah, that's OK," said Heffie. "I'll do them some other time." She slid open the glass door to the refrigerated deli case and grabbed a lone cheese curd, the squiggly shape and bright marigold color of it like a piece from a children's game. She popped it into her mouth. "You ever been surfing?" she asked Jane.

"Surfing?" Jane repeated incredulously. She would never figure out how Heffie came up with the questions she did.

"Yeah. Surfing. You know—some people have done it. The fiberglass board that you stand on in the water and then a wave comes along?" Heffie's face was a snowy moon of things never done.

Jane looked away. "Once a couple of summers ago I went water-skiing on a lake," she said. "In Oregon." Her lover, the daredevil toymaker, had liked to do things like that. "Khem on, Jane," he had said to her. "You only live at once." Which seemed to her all the more reason to be careful, to take it easy, to have an ordinary life. She didn't like to do things where the trick was to not die.

"Water-skiing, poohf," said Heffie. "That's nothing like surfing. There's not the waves, the *risk*." Jane looked up from her clipboard and watched as Heffie waddled away, the tops of her feet swelling out over the straps of her shoes like dough.

Heffie walked over to the Swiss nut rolls, put a fist down lightly on top, and gazed off.

"CARE TO TRY some of our horseradish cheddar today?" Jane smiled and held out the tray. She had placed little teaspoonfuls of spread on some sickly-looking rice crackers, and now she held them out to people like a caterer with the hors d'oeuvres at a fancy party. *Horses' douvers*, her mother used to call them, and for years Jane had had her own idea about what a douver was. "Care to try a free sample of our horseradish cheddar spread, on special today?" At least it wasn't spraying perfume at people. Last month she had met the girl who did that next door at Marshall Field's. The girl, who was from Florida originally, said to her, "Sometimes you *aim* for the eyes. It's not always an accident." Malls, Jane knew, were full of salesgirls with stories. Broken hearts, boyfriends in jail. Once last week two ten-year-old girls, one pudgy, one thin, had come up to Jane, selling chocolate bars. They looked at her as if she were just a taller version of themselves, someone they might turn into when they grew up. "Will you buy a chocolate bar?" they asked her, staring at her samples. Jane offered them a cracker with a big clump of spread, but they politely declined.

"Well, what kind of chocolate bars are you selling?"

"Almond or crisp." The pudgy girl, wearing a purple sweatshirt and lavender corduroys, clutched a worn-out paper bag to her chest.

"Is this for the Girl Scouts?" asked Jane.

The girls looked at each other. "No, it's for my brother," said the pudgy one. Her friend slapped her on the arm.

"It's for your brother's *team*," the friend hissed.

"Yeah," said the girl, and Jane bought a crispy bar and talked them into a sample after all. Which they took with a slight grimace. "D'you got a husband that drives a truck?" asked the one in purple.

"Yeah," said the other. *"Do you?"* And when Jane shook her head, they frowned and went away.

A man in a blue sweater like one her father used to wear stopped and gently plucked a cracker from her tray. "How much?" he asked, and she was about to say, "A million dollars," when she heard someone down the mall corridor call her name.

"Jane Konwicki! How are you?" A woman about Jane's age, wearing a bright-red fall suit, strode up to her and kissed her on the cheek. The man in the blue sweater like her father's slipped away. Jane looked at the woman in the red suit and for a minute didn't know who she was. But the woman's animated features all stopped for a moment and fell into place, and Jane realized it was Bridey, a friend from over fifteen years ago, who used to sit next to her in high school chorus. It was curious how people, when they stood still and you just looked, never really changed that much. No matter how the fashions swirled about a girl, the adult she became, with different fashions swirling about her, still contained the same girl. All of Bridey's ages—the child, the old woman—were there on her face. It was like an open bird feeder where every year of her, the past and the future, had come to feed.

"Bridey, you look great. What have you been up to?" It seemed a ridiculous question to ask of someone you hadn't seen since high school, but there it was.

"Well, last year I fell madly in love," Bridey said with great pride. This clearly was on the top of her list, and her voice suggested it was a long list. "And we got married, and we moved back to town after roughing it on the South Side of Chicago since forever. It's great to be back here, I can tell you." Bridey helped herself to a cheddar sample and then another one. The cheese in her mouth stuck between her front teeth in a pasty, yellowish mortar, and when she swallowed and smiled back at Jane, well, again, there it was, like something unfortunate but necessary.

"You seem so . . . *happy*," said Jane. Heffie was shuffling around noisily in the shop behind her.

"Oh, I am. I keep running into people from school, and it's just so much fun. In fact, Jane, you should come with me this evening. You know what I'm going to do?"

"What?" Jane glanced back over her shoulder and saw Heffie testing the spreads in the deli case with her finger. She would stick her finger in deep and then lick it slowly like an ice cream.

"Oh," said Bridey in a hushed and worried tone. "Is that a customer or an employee?"

"Employee," said Jane.

"At any rate, I'm going to try out for Community Chorus," continued Bridey. "It's part of my new program. I'm learning German—"

"Learning German?" Jane interrupted.

"—taking a cooking class, and I'm going to get back into choral singing."

"You were always a good singer," said Jane. Bridey had often gotten solos.

"Ach! My voice has gone to pot, but I don't care. Why don't you come with me? We could audition together. The auditions aren't supposed to be that hard."

"Oh, I don't know," said Jane, though the thought of singing again in a chorus suddenly excited her. That huge sound flying out over an audience, like a migration of birds, like a million balloons! But the idea of an audition was terrifying. What if she didn't get in? How could she ever open her mouth again to sing, even all by herself at home? How would her own voice not mortify her on the way to work in the morning, when she listened to the radio. Everything would be ruined. Songs would stick in her throat like moths. She would listen to nothing but news, and when she got to work she would be quiet and sad.

"Listen," said Bridey, "I'm terrible. Truly."

"No, you're not. Let me hear you sing something," said Jane.

Bridey looked at her quizzically, took another horseradish cheddar sample, and chewed. "What do you mean? God, these are good."

"I mean just something little. I want to know what you mean by terrible. Cuz *I'm* terrible. Here. I'll get you started. *Row, row, row your boat, gently down the stream . . .*"

"*Merrily, merrily, merrily, merrily,*" continued Bridey rather plainly. Jane wondered whether she was holding back. *"Life is but a dream."* Bridey looked at Jane a little unhappily. "See, I told you I was bad."

"You're much better than I am," said Jane.

"Where are you living now?" Bridey pulled at the red jacket of her suit and looked around the mall.

"Out on Neptune Avenue. Near where it runs into Oak. How about you?"

"We're out in Brickmire Apartments. They have a pool, which is what sold us on the place." Bridey pointed back toward Heffie and whispered, "Does she always go snacking through everything like that?" Bridey had lifted yet another rice cracker from Jane's tray.

"You don't want to know," said Jane.

"You're right. I don't," said Bridey, and she put the rice cracker back on Jane's tray.

AFTER WORK Jane drove back to the west side to pick up her cat at the vet's. She had promised Bridey that she would meet her at the auditions, which were at seven-thirty at their old high school, but her gut buckled at the thought. She tried singing in her car—*Doe, a deer, a female deer*—but her voice sounded hollow and frightened. At a red light someone in the car next to hers saw her lips moving and shook his head.

By the time she got to the vet's, the parking lot was full

of cars. In the waiting room people were collected messily around the front counter, waiting their turn. Two employees behind the counter were doing all the work, one young man at the cash register, and the woman in the white shoes at the microphone, who was saying, "Spotsy Wechsler, Spotsy Wechsler." She put the microphone down. "She'll be right up," she said to a man in a jean jacket a lot like the one Jane's brother had worn all the while they were growing up. "Next?" The woman looked out at the scatter of pet owners in front of her. "Can I help someone?" No one said anything.

"You can help me," said Jane finally, "but this man was here before me. And actually so was he." One of the men ahead of her twisted back to look, red-faced, and then turned front again and spoke very quietly to the woman in the white shoes.

"My name is Miller," said the man, sternly, secretively. He wore a suit, and his tie was loosened. "I'm here to pick up the cat my wife brought in this morning for surgery."

The woman blanched. "Yes," she said, and she didn't ask for a first name. "Gooby Miller," she said into the microphone. "Gooby Miller to the waiting room." The man had taken out his wallet, but the woman said, "No charge," and went over and tapped things into her computer for a very long minute. A young high school kid appeared from the back room, carrying a box in his arms. "The Miller cat?" he said in the doorway, and the man in the suit raised his hand. The boy brought the box over and placed it on the counter.

"I'd also like to speak with the veterinarian," said the man. The woman in the white shoes looked at him fearfully, but the boy said, "Yes, he's waiting for you. Come right this way," and led the man back into the examination room, the door to which blinked brightly open to let them in, then shut behind them like a fact. The box sat all alone on the countertop.

"Can I help you?" the woman asked Jane.

"Yes. I'm here to pick up my cat from the groomer. My name is Konwicki."

The woman reached for the microphone. "And the cat's name?"

"Fluffers," said Jane.

"Fluffers Konwicki to the waiting room." The woman put the microphone down. "The cat'll be up in a minute."

"Thanks," said Jane. She looked at the cardboard box at her elbow on the counter. The box said DOLE PINEAPPLE. She listened for scratching or movement of any kind, but there was none. "What's in the box?" she asked.

The woman made a face, guilty with comedy, exaggerated. She didn't know what sort of face to make. "Gooby Miller," she said. "A dead cat."

"Oh, dear," murmured Jane. She remembered the children she'd met earlier that day. "What happened?"

The woman shrugged. "Thyroid surgery. It just died on the table. Can I help you, sir?" Someone was now bringing out Rex the poodle, who went limping toward his owner with a cast on his front foot. It was all like a dream: Things you'd seen before, in daylight, were trotted out hours later in slightly different form.

After Rex was placed in a child's toy wagon and wheeled out of the vet's, the groomer appeared bearing Fluffers, who looked dazed and smelled of flea dip laced with lilac. "He was a very good cat," said the groomer, and Jane took Fluffers in her arms and almost peeped, "Thank God they didn't bring you out in a pineapple box." What she said instead was: "And now he's all handsome again."

"Found some fleas," said the groomer. "But not all that many."

Jane quickly paid the bill and left. Dusk was settling over the highway like a mood, and the traffic had put on lights. She carried her cat to the car and was fumbling with the door on the passenger's side when she heard squeals from the opposite end of the parking lot. "Fluffers! Fluffers!" They were a child's excited shouts. "Look, it's Fluffers!"

The boy and girl Jane had spoken to that morning suddenly leaped out of the station wagon they'd been waiting in across the lot. They slammed the back doors and dashed breathlessly over to Jane and her cat. They had on little coats and hats with earflaps. It had gotten cold.

"Oh, Fluffers, you smell so good—yum, yum, yum!" said the girl, and she pressed her face into Fluffers' perfumed haunches and kept it there, beginning to cry. Jane looked up and saw that what little light there was left in the sky was frighteningly spindly, like a horse's legs that must somehow still hold up the horse. She freed one of her hands and placed it on the girl's head. "Oh, Fluffers!" came another muffled wail; the girl refused to lift her face. Her brother stood more stoically at her side. His face was pink and swollen, but something was drying hard behind the eyes. He studied Jane as if he were reorganizing what he thought was important in life. "What is your name?" he asked.

IT WAS a little thing, just a little thing, but Jane decided not to risk the audition after all. She phoned Bridey and apologized, said she was coming down with a bug or something, and Bridey said, "Probably got it from that Heffie, always taste-testing the way she does. At any rate, I hope you'll come over for dinner sometime this week, if possible," and Jane said that yes, she would.

And she did. She went the following Thursday and had dinner with Bridey and Bridey's husband, who was a big, gentle man who did consulting work for computer companies. He was wearing a shirt printed with seahorses, like one her ex-lover the toymaker had worn when he had come east to visit, one final weekend, for old times' sake. It had been a beautiful shirt, soft as pajamas, and he'd worn it when they had driven that Sunday, out past the pumpkin fairs, to the state line, to view the Mississippi. The river had rushed by them, beneath them, a clayey green, a deep, deep khaki. She had touched the shirt, held on to it; in this lunarscape of scrub oaks and jack pines, in this place that had once at the start of the world been entirely under water and now just had winds, it was good to have a river cutting through, breaking up the land. In the distance, past a valley dalmatianed with birches, there were larger trees, cedars and goldening tamaracks—goldening!—and Jane felt that at last here was a moment she would take with her into the rest of life, *unlosable*. There seemed nothing so true as a yellow tree.

After dinner she actually went to a Community Chorus rehearsal with Bridey and sang through some of the exercises with everyone. When the sheet music was passed out, however, there wasn't enough to go around. The director took attendance and gazed accusingly out at the sopranos, saying, "Is someone here who isn't actually supposed to be?" Jane raised her hand and explained.

"I'm afraid this is not allowed. If you want to be in the chorus you must have already auditioned."

"I'm sorry," said Jane, and she stood and gave her sheet music back to the choir director. She picked up her purse, looked down at Bridey, and shrugged unhappily.

"I'll phone you," mouthed Bridey.

But it was nearly Christmas season by the time Bridey phoned, and Jane was very busy at the store. There were lots of special holiday dips and cheese rolls, and they were trying to do gift wrap besides. In the midst of it all Heffie announced she was quitting, but the day she did she brought in a bottle of champagne, and she and Jane drank it right there on the job. They poured it into Styrofoam cups and sipped it, crouching behind the deli case, craning their necks occasionally to make sure no customers had wandered in.

"To our little lives," toasted Heffie.

"On the prairie," added Jane. The champagne fizzed against the roof of her mouth. She warmed it there, washing it around, until it flattened, gliding down her throat, a heated, sweet water.

She and Heffie opened a jar of herring in cream sauce, which had a messily torn label. They dug their fingers in and ate. They sang a couple of Christmas carols they both knew, and sang them badly.

"*Let every heart prepare him a room,*" sang Heffie, her mouth full of fish. The world was lovely, really, but it was tricky, and peevish with the small things, like a god who didn't get out much.

"Surfing," said Heffie. "You gotta get away from these plains winters and go someplace with waves and a warm current." Inside the deli case, the dry moons of the cheeses and the mucky spreads wore their usual plastic tags: HELLO MY NAME IS. Jane reached in and plucked out the one that said, HELLO MY NAME IS *Swiss Almond Whip*.

"Here," she said to Heffie. "This is for you." Heffie laughed, gravelly and loud, then took the tag and stuck it in one of her barrettes, up near the front, where the hair was vanishing, and the deforested scalp shone back in surprise, pale but constant, beneath.

# You're
# Ugly,
# Too

YOU HAD TO GET OUT of them occasionally,
those Illinois towns with the funny names: Paris, Oblong, Normal. Once, when the Dow-Jones dipped two hundred points,
the Paris paper boasted a banner headline: NORMAL MAN MAR-
RIES OBLONG WOMAN. They knew what was important. They
did! But you had to get out once in a while, even if it was just
across the border to Terre Haute, for a movie.

Outside of Paris, in the middle of a large field, was a scatter
of brick buildings, a small liberal arts college with the im-
probable name of Hilldale-Versailles. Zoë Hendricks had been
teaching American History there for three years. She taught
"The Revolution and Beyond" to freshmen and sophomores,
and every third semester she had the Senior Seminar for Majors,
and although her student evaluations had been slipping in the
last year and a half—*Professor Hendricks is often late for class and
usually arrives with a cup of hot chocolate, which she offers the class
sips of*—generally, the department of nine men was pleased to
have her. They felt she added some needed feminine touch to
the corridors—that faint trace of Obsession and sweat, the light,
fast clicking of heels. Plus they had had a sex-discrimination
suit, and the dean had said, well, it was time.

The situation was not easy for her, they knew. Once, at the
start of last semester, she had skipped into her lecture hall

singing "Getting to Know You"—both verses. At the request of the dean, the chairman had called her into his office, but did not ask her for an explanation, not really. He asked her how she was and then smiled in an avuncular way. She said, "Fine," and he studied the way she said it, her front teeth catching on the inside of her lower lip. She was almost pretty, but her face showed the strain and ambition of always having been close but not quite. There was too much effort with the eyeliner, and her earrings, worn no doubt for the drama her features lacked, were a little frightening, jutting out from the side of her head like antennae.

"I'm going out of my mind," said Zoë to her younger sister, Evan, in Manhattan. *Professor Hendricks seems to know the entire sound track to* The King and I. *Is this history?* Zoë phoned her every Tuesday.

"You always say that," said Evan, "but then you go on your trips and vacations and then you settle back into things and then you're quiet for a while and then you say you're fine, you're busy, and then after a while you say you're going crazy again, and you start all over." Evan was a part-time food designer for photo shoots. She cooked vegetables in green dye. She propped up beef stew with a bed of marbles and shopped for new kinds of silicone sprays and plastic ice cubes. She thought her life was "OK." She was living with her boyfriend of many years, who was independently wealthy and had an amusing little job in book publishing. They were five years out of college, and they lived in a luxury midtown high-rise with a balcony and access to a pool. "It's not the same as having your own pool," Evan was always sighing, as if to let Zoë know that, as with Zoë, there were still things she, Evan, had to do without.

"Illinois. It makes me sarcastic to be here," said Zoë on the phone. She used to insist it was irony, something gently layered and sophisticated, something alien to the Midwest, but her students kept calling it sarcasm, something they felt qualified to recognize, and now she had to agree. It wasn't irony. *What is your perfume?* a student once asked her. *Room freshener*, she said. She smiled, but he looked at her, unnerved.

Her students were by and large good Midwesterners, spacey with estrogen from large quantities of meat and cheese. They shared their parents' suburban values; their parents had given them things, things, things. They were complacent. They had been purchased. They were armed with a healthy vagueness about anything historical or geographic. They seemed actually to know very little about anything, but they were extremely good-natured about it. "All those states in the East are so tiny and jagged and bunched up," complained one of her undergraduates the week she was lecturing on "The Turning Point of Independence: The Battle at Saratoga." "Professor Hendricks, you're from Delaware originally, right?" the student asked her.

"Maryland," corrected Zoë.

"Aw," he said, waving his hand dismissively. "New England."

Her articles—chapters toward a book called *Hearing the One About: Uses of Humor in the American Presidency*—were generally well received, though they came slowly for her. She liked her pieces to have something from every time of day in them—she didn't trust things written in the morning only—so she reread and rewrote painstakingly. No part of a day, its moods, its light, was allowed to dominate. She hung on to a piece for over a year sometimes, revising at all hours, until the entirety of a day had registered there.

The job she'd had before the one at Hilldale-Versailles had been at a small college in New Geneva, Minnesota, Land of the Dying Shopping Mall. Everyone was so blond there that brunettes were often presumed to be from foreign countries. *Just because Professor Hendricks is from Spain doesn't give her the right to be so negative about our country.* There was a general emphasis on cheerfulness. In New Geneva you weren't supposed to be critical or complain. You weren't supposed to notice that the town had overextended and that its shopping malls were raggedy and going under. You were never to say you weren't fine thank you and yourself. You were supposed to be Heidi. You were supposed to lug goat milk up the hills and not think twice. Heidi did not complain. Heidi did not do things like stand in front of the new IBM photocopier, saying, "If this fucking Xerox machine breaks on me one more time, I'm going to slit my wrists."

But now, in her second job, in her fourth year of teaching in the Midwest, Zoë was discovering something she never suspected she had: a crusty edge, brittle and pointed. Once she had pampered her students, singing them songs, letting them call her at home, even, and ask personal questions. Now she was losing sympathy. They were beginning to seem different. They were beginning to seem demanding and spoiled.

"You act," said one of her Senior Seminar students at a scheduled conference, "like your opinion is worth more than everybody else's in the class."

Zoë's eyes widened. "I *am* the teacher," she said. "I *do* get paid to act like that." She narrowed her gaze at the student, who was wearing a big leather bow in her hair, like a cowgirl in a TV ranch show. "I mean, otherwise *everybody* in the class would have little offices and office hours." *Sometimes Professor Hendricks will take up the class's time just talking about movies she's seen.* She stared at the student some more, then added, "I bet you'd like that."

"Maybe I sound whiny to you," said the girl, "but I simply want my history major to mean something."

"Well, there's your problem," said Zoë, and with a smile, she showed the student to the door. "I like your bow," she added.

Zoë lived for the mail, for the postman, that handsome blue jay, and when she got a real letter, with a real full-price stamp, from someplace else, she took it to bed with her and read it over and over. She also watched television until all hours and had her set in the bedroom, a bad sign. *Professor Hendricks has said critical things about Fawn Hall, the Catholic religion, and the whole state of Illinois. It is unbelievable.* At Christmastime she gave twenty-dollar tips to the mailman and to Jerry, the only cabbie in town, whom she had gotten to know from all her rides to and from the Terre Haute airport, and who, since he realized such rides were an extravagance, often gave her cut rates.

"I'm flying in to visit you this weekend," announced Zoë.

"I was hoping you would," said Evan. "Charlie and I are having a party for Halloween. It'll be fun."

"I have a costume already. It's a bonehead. It's this thing that looks like a giant bone going through your head."

"Great," said Evan.

"It is, it's great."

"Alls I have is my moon mask from last year and the year before. I'll probably end up getting married in it."

"Are you and Charlie getting *married?*" Foreboding filled her voice.

"Hmmmmmmmnnno, not immediately."

"Don't get married."

"Why?"

"Just not yet. You're too young."

"You're only saying that because you're five years older than I am and *you're* not married."

"*I'm* not married? Oh, my God," said Zoë. "I forgot to get married."

Zoë had been out with three men since she'd come to Hilldale-Versailles. One of them was a man in the Paris municipal bureaucracy who had fixed a parking ticket she'd brought in to protest and who then asked her to coffee. At first she thought he was amazing—at last, someone who did not want

Heidi! But soon she came to realize that all men, deep down, wanted Heidi. Heidi with cleavage. Heidi with outfits. The parking ticket bureaucrat soon became tired and intermittent. One cool fall day, in his snazzy, impractical convertible, when she asked him what was wrong, he said, "You would not be ill-served by new clothes, you know." She wore a lot of gray-green corduroy. She had been under the impression that it brought out her eyes, those shy stars. She flicked an ant from her sleeve.

"Did you have to brush that off in the car?" he said, driving. He glanced down at his own pectorals, giving first the left, then the right, a quick survey. He was wearing a tight shirt.

"Excuse me?"

He slowed down at a yellow light and frowned. "Couldn't you have picked it up and thrown it outside?"

"The ant? It might have bitten me. I mean, what difference does it make?"

"It might have bitten you! Ha! How ridiculous! Now it's going to lay eggs in my car!"

The second guy was sweeter, lunkier, though not insensitive to certain paintings and songs, but too often, too, things he'd do or say would startle her. Once, in a restaurant, he stole the garnishes off her dinner plate and waited for her to notice. When she didn't, he finally thrust his fist across the table and said, "Look," and when he opened it, there was her parsley sprig and her orange slice, crumpled to a wad. Another time he described to her his recent trip to the Louvre. "And there I was in front of Géricault's *Raft of the Medusa*, and everyone else had wandered off, so I had my own private audience with it, all those painted, drowning bodies splayed in every direction, and there's this motion in that painting that starts at the bottom left, swirling and building, and building, and building, and going up to the right-hand corner, where there's this guy waving a flag, and on the horizon in the distance you could see this teeny tiny boat. . . ." He was breathless in the telling. She found this touching and smiled in encouragement. "A painting like that," he said, shaking his head. "It just makes you shit."

"I have to ask you something," said Evan. "I know every woman complains about not meeting men, but really, on my shoots, I meet a lot of men. And they're not all gay, either." She paused. "Not anymore."

"What are you asking?"

The third guy was a political science professor named Murray Peterson, who liked to go out on double dates with colleagues whose wives he was attracted to. Usually the wives would consent to flirt with him. Under the table sometimes there was footsie, and once there was even kneesie. Zoë and the husband would be left to their food, staring into their water glasses, chewing like goats. "Oh, Murray," said one wife, who had never finished her master's in physical therapy and wore great clothes. "You know, I know everything about you: your birthday, your license plate number. I have everything memorized. But then that's the kind of mind I have. Once at a dinner party I amazed the host by getting up and saying good-bye to every single person there, first *and* last names."

"I knew a dog who could do that," said Zoë, with her mouth full. Murray and the wife looked at her with vexed and rebuking expressions, but the husband seemed suddenly twinkling and amused. Zoë swallowed. "It was a Talking Lab, and after about ten minutes of listening to the dinner conversation this dog knew everyone's name. You could say, 'Bring this knife to Murray Peterson,' and it would."

"Really," said the wife, frowning, and Murray Peterson never called again.

"Are you seeing anyone?" said Evan. "I'm asking for a particular reason, I'm not just being like mom."

"I'm seeing my house. I'm tending to it when it wets, when it cries, when it throws up." Zoë had bought a mint-green ranch house near campus, though now she was thinking that maybe she shouldn't have. It was hard to live in a house. She kept wandering in and out of the rooms, wondering where she had put things. She went downstairs into the basement for no reason at all except that it amused her to own a basement. It also amused her to own a tree. The day she moved in, she had tacked to her tree a small paper sign that said *Zoë's Tree*.

Her parents, in Maryland, had been very pleased that one of their children had at last been able to afford real estate, and when she closed on the house they sent her flowers with a Congratulations card. Her mother had even UPS'd a box of old decorating magazines saved over the years, photographs of beautiful rooms her mother used to moon over, since there never had been any money to redecorate. It was like getting her mother's pornography, that box, inheriting her drooled-upon fantasies, the endless wish and tease that had been her life. But to her mother it was a rite of passage that pleased her. "Maybe you will get some ideas from these," she had written. And when Zoë looked at the photographs, at the bold and beautiful living rooms, she was filled with longing. Ideas and ideas of longing.

Right now Zoë's house was rather empty. The previous owner had wallpapered around the furniture, leaving strange gaps and silhouettes on the walls, and Zoë hadn't done much about that yet. She had bought furniture, then taken it back, furnishing and unfurnishing, preparing and shedding, like a womb. She had bought several plain pine chests to use as love seats or boot boxes, but they came to look to her more and more like children's coffins, so she returned them. And she had recently bought an Oriental rug for the living room, with Chinese symbols on it she didn't understand. The salesgirl had kept saying she was sure they meant *Peace* and *Eternal Life*, but when Zoë got the rug home, she worried. What if they didn't mean *Peace* and *Eternal Life*? What if they meant, say, *Bruce Springsteen*. And the more she thought about it, the more she became convinced she had a rug that said *Bruce Springsteen*, and so she returned that, too.

She had also bought a little baroque mirror for the front entryway, which she had been told, by Murray Peterson, would keep away evil spirits. The mirror, however, tended to frighten *her*, startling her with an image of a woman she never recognized. Sometimes she looked puffier and plainer than she remembered. Sometimes shifty and dark. Most times she just looked vague. *You look like someone I know*, she had been told twice in the last year by strangers in restaurants in Terre Haute. In fact, sometimes she seemed not to have a look of her own, or any look whatsoever, and it began to amaze her that her students and colleagues were able to recognize her at all. How did they know? When she walked into a room, how did she look so that they knew it was her? Like this? Did she look like this? And so she returned the mirror.

"The reason I'm asking is that I know a man I think you should meet," said Evan. "He's fun. He's straight. He's single. That's all I'm going to say."

"I think I'm too old for fun," said Zoë. She had a dark bristly hair in her chin, and she could feel it now with her finger. Perhaps when you had been without the opposite sex for too long, you began to resemble them. In an act of desperate invention, you began to grow your own. "I just want to come, wear my bonehead, visit with Charlie's tropical fish, ask you about your food shoots."

She thought about all the papers on "Our Constitution: How It Affects Us" she was going to have to correct. She thought about how she was going in for ultrasound tests on Friday, because, according to her doctor and her doctor's assistant, she had a large, mysterious growth in her abdomen. Gallbladder, they kept saying. Or ovaries or colon. "You guys practice medicine?" asked Zoë, aloud, after they had left the room. Once, as a girl, she brought her dog to a vet, who had told her, "Well, either your dog has worms or cancer or else it was hit by a car."

She was looking forward to New York.

"Well, whatever. We'll just play it cool. I can't wait to see you, hon. Don't forget your bonehead," said Evan.

"A bonehead you don't forget," said Zoë.

"I suppose," said Evan.

The ultrasound Zoë was keeping a secret, even from Evan. "I feel like I'm dying," Zoë had hinted just once on the phone.

"You're not dying," said Evan. "You're just annoyed."

"Ultrasound," Zoë now said jokingly to the technician who put the cold jelly on her bare stomach. "Does that sound like a really great stereo system, or what?" She had not had anyone make this much fuss over her bare stomach since her boyfriend in graduate school, who had hovered over her whenever she felt ill, waved his arms, pressed his hands upon her navel, and drawled evangelically, "Heal! Heal for thy Baby Jesus' sake!" Zoë would laugh and they would make love, both secretly hoping she would get pregnant. Later they would worry together, and he would sink a cheek to her belly and ask whether she was late, was she late, was she sure, she might be late, and when after two years she had not gotten pregnant, they took to quarreling and drifted apart.

"OK," said the technician absently.

The monitor was in place, and Zoë's insides came on the screen in all their gray and ribbony hollowness. They were marbled in the finest gradations of black and white, like stone in an old church or a picture of the moon. "Do you suppose," she babbled at the technician, "that the rise in infertility among so many couples in this country is due to completely different species trying to reproduce?" The technician moved the scanner around and took more pictures. On one view in particular, on Zoë's right side, the technician became suddenly alert, the machine he was operating clicking away.

Zoë stared at the screen. "That must be the growth you found there," suggested Zoë.

"I can't tell you anything," said the technician rigidly. "Your doctor will get the radiologist's report this afternoon and will phone you then."

"I'll be out of town," said Zoë.

"I'm sorry," said the technician.

Driving home, Zoë looked in the rearview mirror and decided she looked—well, how would one describe it? A little wan. She thought of the joke about the guy who visits his doctor and the doctor says, "Well, I'm sorry to say you've got six weeks to live."

"I want a second opinion," says the guy. *You act like your opinion is worth more than everyone else's in the class.*

"You want a second opinion? OK," says the doctor. "You're ugly, too." She liked that joke. She thought it was terribly, terribly funny.

She took a cab to the airport, Jerry the cabbie happy to see her.

"Have fun in New York," he said, getting her bag out of the trunk. He liked her, or at least he always acted as if he did. She called him "Jare."

"Thanks, Jare."

"You know, I'll tell you a secret: I've never been to New York. I'll tell you two secrets: I've never been on a plane." And he waved at her sadly as she pushed her way in through the terminal door. "Or an escalator!" he shouted.

The trick to flying safe, Zoë always said, was never to buy a discount ticket and to tell yourself you had nothing to live for anyway, so that when the plane crashed it was no big deal. Then, when it didn't crash, when you had succeeded in keeping it aloft with your own worthlessness, all you had to do was stagger off, locate your luggage, and, by the time a cab arrived, come up with a persuasive reason to go on living.

"YOU'RE HERE!" shrieked Evan over the doorbell, before she even opened the door. Then she opened it wide. Zoë set her bags on the hall floor and hugged Evan hard. When she was little, Evan had always been affectionate and devoted. Zoë had always taken care of her, advising, reassuring, until recently, when it seemed Evan had started advising and reassuring *her*. It startled Zoë. She suspected it had something to do with Zoë's being alone. It made people uncomfortable. "How *are* you?"

"I threw up on on the plane. Besides that, I'm OK."

"Can I get you something? Here, let me take your suitcase. Sick on the plane. Eeeyew."

"It was into one of those sickness bags," said Zoë, just in case Evan thought she'd lost it in the aisle. "I was very quiet."

The apartment was spacious and bright, with a view all the way downtown along the East Side. There was a balcony and sliding glass doors. "I keep forgetting how nice this apartment is. Twentieth floor, doorman . . ." Zoë could work her whole life and never have an apartment like this. So could Evan. It was Charlie's apartment. He and Evan lived in it like two kids in a dorm, beer cans and clothes strewn around. Evan put Zoë's bag away from the mess, over by the fish tank. "I'm so glad you're here," she said. "Now what can I get you?"

Evan made them a snack—soup from a can, and saltines.

"I don't know about Charlie," she said, after they had finished. "I feel like we've gone all sexless and middle-aged already."

"Hmmm," said Zoë. She leaned back into Evan's sofa and stared out the window at the dark tops of the buildings. It seemed a little unnatural to live up in the sky like this, like birds that out of some wrongheaded derring-do had nested too high. She nodded toward the lighted fish tanks and giggled.

"I feel like a bird," she said, "with my own personal supply of fish."

Evan sighed. "He comes home and just sacks out on the sofa, watching fuzzy football. He's wearing the psychic cold cream and curlers, if you know what I mean."

Zoë sat up, readjusted the sofa cushions. "What's fuzzy football?"

"We haven't gotten cable yet. Everything comes in fuzzy. Charlie just watches it that way."

"Hmmm, yeah, that's a little depressing," Zoë said. She looked at her hands. "Especially the part about not having cable."

"This is how he gets into bed at night." Evan stood up to demonstrate. "He whips all his clothes off, and when he gets to his underwear, he lets it drop to one ankle. Then he kicks up his leg and flips the underwear in the air and catches it. I, of course, watch from the bed. There's nothing else. There's just that."

"Maybe you should just get it over with and get married."

"Really?"

"Yeah. I mean, you guys probably think living together like this is the best of both worlds, but . . ." Zoë tried to sound like an older sister; an older sister was supposed to be the parent you could never have, the hip, cool mom. ". . . I've always found that as soon as you think you've got the best of both worlds"—she thought now of herself, alone in her house; of the toad-faced cicadas that flew around like little caped men at night, landing on her screens, staring; of the size fourteen shoes she placed at the doorstep, to scare off intruders; of the ridiculous inflatable blow-up doll someone had told her to keep propped up at the breakfast table—"it can suddenly twist and become the worst of both worlds."

"Really?" Evan was beaming. "Oh, Zoë. I have something to tell you. Charlie and I *are* getting married."

"Really." Zoë felt confused.

"I didn't know how to tell you."

"Yes, well, I guess the part about fuzzy football misled me a little."

"I was hoping you'd be my maid of honor," said Evan, waiting. "Aren't you happy for me?"

"Yes," said Zoë, and she began to tell Evan a story about an award-winning violinist at Hilldale-Versailles, how the violinist had come home from a competition in Europe and taken up with a local man, who made her go to all his summer softball games, made her cheer for him from the stands, with the wives, until she later killed herself. But when she got halfway through, to the part about cheering at the softball games, Zoë stopped.

"What?" said Evan. "So what happened?"

"Actually, nothing," said Zoë lightly. "She just really got into softball. I mean, really. You should have seen her."

ZOË DECIDED to go to a late-afternoon movie, leaving Evan to chores she needed to do before the party—*I have to do them alone*, she'd said, a little tense after the violinist story. Zoë thought about going to an art museum, but women alone in art museums had to look good. They always did. Chic and serious, moving languidly, with a great handbag. Instead, she walked over and down through Kips Bay, past an earring boutique called Stick It in Your Ear, past a beauty salon called Dorian Gray's. That was the funny thing about *beauty*, thought Zoë. Look it up in the yellow pages, and you found a hundred entries, hostile with wit, cutesy with warning. But look up *truth*—ha! There was nothing at all.

Zoë thought about Evan getting married. Would Evan turn into Peter Pumpkin Eater's wife? Mrs. Eater? At the wedding would she make Zoë wear some flouncy lavender dress, identical with the other maids'? Zoë hated uniforms, had even, in the first grade, refused to join Elf Girls, because she didn't want to wear the same dress as everyone else. Now she might have to. But maybe she could distinguish it. Hitch it up on one side with a clothespin. Wear surgical gauze at the waist. Clip to her bodice one of those pins that said in loud letters, SHIT HAPPENS.

At the movie—*Death by Number*—she bought strands of red licorice to tug and chew. She took a seat off to one side in the theater. She felt strangely self-conscious sitting alone and hoped for the place to darken fast. When it did, and the coming attractions came on, she reached inside her purse for her glasses. They were in a Baggie. Her Kleenex was also in a Baggie. So were her pen and her aspirin and her mints. Everything was in Baggies. This was what she'd become: *a woman alone at the movies with everything in a Baggie.*

AT THE HALLOWEEN PARTY, there were about two dozen people. There were people with ape heads and large hairy hands. There was someone dressed as a leprechaun. There was someone dressed as a frozen dinner. Some man had brought his two small daughters: a ballerina and a ballerina's sister, also dressed as a ballerina. There was a gaggle of sexy witches—women dressed entirely in black, beautifully made up and jeweled. "I hate those sexy witches. It's not in the spirit of Halloween," said Evan. Evan had abandoned the moon mask and dolled herself up as a hausfrau, in curlers and an apron, a decision she now regretted. Charlie, because he liked fish, because he owned fish, collected fish, had decided to go as a fish. He had fins and eyes on the side of his head. "Zoë! How are you! I'm sorry I wasn't here when you first arrived!" He spent the rest of his time chatting up the sexy witches.

"Isn't there something I can help you with here?" Zoë asked her sister. "You've been running yourself ragged." She rubbed her sister's arm, gently, as if she wished they were alone.

"Oh, God, not at all," said Evan, arranging stuffed mushrooms on a plate. The timer went off, and she pulled another sheetful out of the oven. "Actually, you know what you can do?"

"What?" Zoë put on her bonehead.

"Meet Earl. He's the guy I had in mind for you. When he gets here, just talk to him a little. He's nice. He's fun. He's going through a divorce."

"I'll try." Zoë groaned. "OK? I'll try." She looked at her watch.

When Earl arrived, he was dressed as a naked woman, steel wool glued strategically to a body stocking, and large rubber breasts protruding like hams.

"Zoë, this is Earl," said Evan.

"Good to meet you," said Earl, circling Evan to shake Zoë's hand. He stared at the top of Zoë's head. "Great bone."

Zoë nodded. "Great tits," she said. She looked past him, out the window at the city thrown glitteringly up against the sky; people were saying the usual things: how it looked like jewels, like bracelets and necklaces unstrung. You could see Grand Central station, the clock of the Con Ed building, the red-and-gold-capped Empire State, the Chrysler like a rocket ship dreamed up in a depression. Far west you could glimpse the Astor Plaza, its flying white roof like a nun's habit. "There's beer out on the balcony, Earl—can I get you one?" Zoë asked.

"Sure, uh, I'll come along. Hey, Charlie, how's it going?"

Charlie grinned and whistled. People turned to look. "Hey, Earl," someone called, from across the room. "Va-va-va-voom."

They squeezed their way past the other guests, past the apes and the sexy witches. The suction of the sliding door gave way in a whoosh, and Zoë and Earl stepped out onto the balcony, a bonehead and a naked woman, the night air roaring and smoky cool. Another couple was out here, too, murmuring privately.

They were not wearing costumes. They smiled at Zoë and Earl. "Hi," said Zoë. She found the plastic-foam cooler, dug into it, and retrieved two beers.

"Thanks," said Earl. His rubber breasts folded inward, dimpled and dented, as he twisted open the bottle.

"Well," sighed Zoë anxiously. She had to learn not to be afraid of a man, the way, in your childhood, you learned not to be afraid of an earthworm or a bug. Often, when she spoke to men at parties, she rushed things in her mind. As the man politely blathered on, she would fall in love, marry, then find herself in a bitter custody battle with him for the kids and hoping for a reconciliation, so that despite all his betrayals she might no longer despise him, and in the few minutes remaining, learn, perhaps, what his last name was and what he did for a living, though probably there was already too much history between them. She would nod, blush, turn away.

"Evan tells me you're a professor. Where do you teach?"

"Just over the Indiana border into Illinois."

He looked a little shocked. "I guess Evan didn't tell me that part."

"She didn't?"

"No."

"Well, that's Evan for you. When we were kids we both had speech impediments."

"That can be tough," said Earl. One of his breasts was hidden behind his drinking arm, but the other shone low and pink, full as a strawberry moon.

"Yes, well, it wasn't a total loss. We used to go to what we called peach pearapy. For about ten years of my life I had to map out every sentence in my mind, way ahead, before I said it. That was the only way I could get a coherent sentence out."

Earl drank from his beer. "How did you do that? I mean, how did you get through?"

"I told a lot of jokes. Jokes you know the lines to already—you can just say them. I love jokes. Jokes and songs."

Earl smiled. He had on lipstick, a deep shade of red, but it was wearing off from the beer. "What's your favorite joke?"

"Uh, my favorite joke is probably . . . OK, all right. This guy goes into a doctor's office and—"

"I think I know this one," interrupted Earl, eagerly. He wanted to tell it himself. "A guy goes into a doctor's office, and the doctor tells him he's got some good news and some bad news—that one, right?"

"I'm not sure," said Zoë. "This might be a different version."

"So the guy says, 'Give me the bad news first,' and the doctor says, 'OK. You've got three weeks to live.' And the guy cries, 'Three weeks to live! Doctor, what is the good news?' And the doctor says, 'Did you see that secretary out front? I finally fucked her.' "

Zoë frowned.

"That's not the one you were thinking of?"

"No." There was accusation in her voice. "Mine was different."

"Oh," said Earl. He looked away and then back again. "You teach history, right? What kind of history do you teach?"

"I teach American, mostly—eighteenth and nineteenth century." In graduate school, at bars, the pickup line was always: "So what's your century?"

"Occasionally I teach a special theme course," she added, "say, 'Humor and Personality in the White House.' That's what my book's on." She thought of something someone once told her about bowerbirds, how they build elaborate structures before mating.

"Your book's on *humor?*"

"Yeah, and, well, when I teach a theme course like that, I do all the centuries." *So what's your century?*

"All three of them."

"Pardon?" The breeze glistened her eyes. Traffic revved beneath them. She felt high and puny, like someone lifted into heaven by mistake and then spurned.

"Three. There's only three."

"Well, four, really." She was thinking of Jamestown, and of the Pilgrims coming here with buckles and witch hats to say their prayers.

"I'm a photographer," said Earl. His face was starting to gleam, his rouge smearing in a sunset beneath his eyes.

"Do you like that?"

"Well, actually I'm starting to feel it's a little dangerous."

"Really?"

"Spending all your time in a darkroom with that red light and all those chemicals. There's links with Parkinson's, you know."

"No, I didn't."

"I suppose I should wear rubber gloves, but I don't like to. Unless I'm touching it directly, I don't think of it as real."

"Hmmm," said Zoë. Alarm buzzed through her, mildly, like a tea.

"Sometimes, when I have a cut or something, I feel the sting and think, *Shit*. I wash constantly and just hope. I don't like rubber over the skin like that."

"Really."

"I mean, the physical contact. That's what you want, or why bother?"

"I guess," said Zoë. She wished she could think of a joke, something slow and deliberate, with the end in sight. She thought of gorillas, how when they had been kept too long alone in cages, they would smack each other in the head instead of mating.

"Are you . . . in a relationship?" Earl suddenly blurted.

"Now? As we speak?"

"Well, I mean, I'm sure you have a relationship to your *work*." A smile, a weird one, nestled in his mouth like an egg. She thought of zoos in parks, how when cities were under siege, during world wars, people ate the animals. "But I mean, with a *man*."

"No, I'm not in a relationship with a *man*." She rubbed her chin with her hand and could feel the one bristly hair there. "But my last relationship was with a very sweet man," she said. She made something up. "From Switzerland. He was a botanist—a weed expert. His name was Jerry. I called him 'Jare.' He was so funny. You'd go to the movies with him and all he would notice were the plants. He would never pay attention to the plot. Once, in a jungle movie, he started rattling off all these Latin names, out loud. It was very exciting for him." She paused, caught her breath. "Eventually he went back to Europe to, uh, study the edelweiss." She looked at Earl. "Are you involved in a relationship? With a *woman?*"

Earl shifted his weight, and the creases in his body stocking changed, splintering outward like something broken. His pubic hair slid over to one hip, like a corsage on a saloon girl. "No," he said, clearing his throat. The steel wool in his underarms was inching toward his biceps. "I've just gotten out of a marriage that was full of bad dialogue, like 'You want more *space?* I'll give you more space!' *Clonk.* Your basic Three Stooges."

Zoë looked at him sympathetically. "I suppose it's hard for love to recover after that."

His eyes lit up. He wanted to talk about love. "But *I* keep thinking love should be like a tree. You look at trees and they've got bumps and scars from tumors, infestations, what have you, but they're still growing. Despite the bumps and bruises, they're . . . straight."

"Yeah, well," said Zoë, "where I'm from, they're all married or gay. Did you see that movie *Death by Number?*"

Earl looked at her, a little lost. She was getting away from him. "No," he said.

One of his breasts had slipped under his arm, tucked there like a baguette. She kept thinking of trees, of gorillas and parks, of people in wartime eating the zebras. She felt a stabbing pain in her abdomen.

"Want some hors d'oeuvres?" Evan came pushing through the sliding door. She was smiling, though her curlers were coming out, hanging bedraggled at the ends of her hair like Christmas decorations, like food put out for the birds. She thrust forward a plate of stuffed mushrooms.

"Are you asking for donations or giving them away," said Earl, wittily. He liked Evan, and he put his arm around her.

"You know, I'll be right back," said Zoë.

"Oh," said Evan, looking concerned.

"Right back. I promise."

Zoë hurried inside, across the living room, into the bedroom, to the adjoining bath. It was empty; most of the guests were using the half bath near the kitchen. She flicked on the light and closed the door. The pain had stopped and she didn't really have to go to the bathroom, but she stayed there anyway, resting. In the mirror above the sink she looked haggard beneath her bonehead, violet grays showing under the skin like a plucked and pocky bird. She leaned closer, raising her chin a little to find the bristly hair. It was there, at the end of the jaw, sharp and dark as a wire. She opened the medicine cabinet, pawed through it until she found some tweezers. She lifted her head again and poked at her face with the metal tips, grasping and pinching and missing. Outside the door she could hear two people talking low. They had come into the bedroom and were discussing something. They were sitting on the bed. One of them giggled in a false way. She stabbed again at her chin, and it started to bleed a little. She pulled the skin tight along the jawbone, gripped the tweezers hard around what she hoped was the hair, and tugged. A tiny square of skin came away with it, but the hair remained, blood bright at the root of it. Zoë clenched her teeth. "Come on," she whispered. The couple outside in the bedroom were now telling stories, softly, and laughing. There was a bounce and squeak of mattress, and the sound of a chair being moved out of the way. Zoë aimed the tweezers carefully, pinched, then pulled gently away, and this time the hair came, too, with a slight twinge of pain and then a great flood of relief. "Yeah!" breathed Zoë. She grabbed some toilet paper and dabbed at her chin. It came away spotted with blood, and so she tore off some more and pressed hard until it stopped. Then she turned off the light and opened the door, to return to the party. "Excuse me," she said to the couple in the bedroom. They were the couple from the balcony, and they looked at her, a bit surprised. They had their arms around each other, and they were eating candy bars.

Earl was still out on the balcony, alone, and Zoë rejoined him there.

"Hi," she said. He turned around and smiled. He had straightened his costume out a bit, though all the secondary sex characteristics seemed slightly doomed, destined to shift and flip and zip around again any moment.

"Are you OK?" he asked. He had opened another beer and was chugging.

"Oh, yeah. I just had to go to the bathroom." She paused. "Actually I have been going to a lot of doctors recently."

"What's wrong?" asked Earl.

"Oh, probably nothing. But they're putting me through tests." She sighed. "I've had sonograms. I've had mammograms. Next week I'm going in for a candygram." He looked at her worriedly. "I've had too many gram words," she said.

"Here, I saved you these." He held out a napkin with two

stuffed mushroom caps. They were cold and leaving oil marks on the napkin.

"Thanks," said Zoë, and pushed them both in her mouth. "Watch," she said, with her mouth full. "With my luck, it'll be a gallbladder operation."

Earl made a face. "So your sister's getting married," he said, changing the subject. "Tell me, really, what you think about love."

"*Love?*" Hadn't they done this already? "I don't know." She chewed thoughtfully and swallowed. "All right. I'll tell you what I think about love. Here is a love story. This friend of mine—"

"You've got something on your chin," said Earl, and he reached over to touch it.

"*What?*" said Zoë, stepping back. She turned her face away and grabbed at her chin. A piece of toilet paper peeled off it, like tape. "It's nothing," she said. "It's just—it's nothing."

Earl stared at her.

"At any rate," she continued, "this friend of mine was this award-winning violinist. She traveled all over Europe and won competitions; she made records, she gave concerts, she got famous. But she had no social life. So one day she threw herself at the feet of this conductor she had a terrible crush on. He picked her up, scolded her gently, and sent her back to her hotel room. After that she came home from Europe. She went back to her old hometown, stopped playing the violin, and took up with a local boy. This was in Illinois. He took her to some Big Ten bar every night to drink with his buddies from the team. He used to say things like "Katrina here likes to play the violin," and then he'd pinch her cheek. When she once suggested that they go home, he said, 'What, you think you're too famous for a place like this? Well, let me tell you something. You may think you're famous, but you're not *famous* famous.'

Two famouses. 'No one here's ever heard of you.' Then he went up and bought a round of drinks for everyone but her. She got her coat, went home, and shot a gun through her head."

Earl was silent.

"That's the end of my love story," said Zoë.

"You're not at all like your sister," said Earl.

"Ho, really," said Zoë. The air had gotten colder, the wind singing minor and thick as a dirge.

"No." He didn't want to talk about love anymore. "You know, you should wear a lot of blue—blue and white—around your face. It would bring out your coloring." He reached an arm out to show her how the blue bracelet he was wearing might look against her skin, but she swatted it away.

"Tell me, Earl. Does the word *fag* mean anything to you?"

He stepped back, away from her. He shook his head in disbelief. "You know, I just shouldn't try to go out with career women. You're all stricken. A guy can really tell what life has done to you. I do better with women who have part-time jobs."

"Oh, yes?" said Zoë. She had once read an article entitled "Professional Women and the Demographics of Grief." Or no, it was a poem: *If there were a lake, the moonlight would dance across it in conniptions.* She remembered that line. But perhaps the title was "The Empty House: Aesthetics of Barrenness." Or maybe "Space Gypsies: Girls in Academe." She had forgotten.

Earl turned and leaned on the railing of the balcony. It was getting late. Inside, the party guests were beginning to leave. The sexy witches were already gone. "Live and learn," Earl murmured.

"Live and get dumb," replied Zoë. Beneath them on Lexington there were no cars, just the gold rush of an occasional cab. He leaned hard on his elbows, brooding.

"Look at those few people down there," he said. "They look like bugs. You know how bugs are kept under control? They're sprayed with bug hormones, female bug hormones. The male bugs get so crazy in the presence of this hormone, they're screwing everything in sight: trees, rocks—everything but female bugs. Population control. That's what's happening in this country," he said drunkenly. "Hormones sprayed around, and now men are screwing rocks. Rocks!"

In the back the Magic Marker line of his buttocks spread wide, a sketchy black on pink like a funnies page. Zoë came up, slow, from behind and gave him a shove. His arms slipped forward, off the railing, out over the street. Beer spilled out of his bottle, raining twenty stories down to the street.

"Hey, what are you doing?!" he said, whipping around. He stood straight and readied and moved away from the railing, sidestepping Zoë. "What the *hell* are you doing?"

"Just kidding," she said. "I was just kidding." But he gazed at her, appalled and frightened, his Magic Marker buttocks turned away now toward all of downtown, a naked pseudo-woman with a blue bracelet at the wrist, trapped out on a balcony with—with *what? "Really, I was just kidding!"* Zoë shouted. The wind lifted the hair up off her head, skyward in spines behind the bone. If there were a lake, the moonlight would dance across it in conniptions. She smiled at him, and wondered how she looked.

# Places
# to Look
# for Your Mind

THE SIGN SAID "WELCOME TO AMERICA," in bold red letters. Underneath, in smaller blue, Millie had spelled out *John Spee*. Comma, *John Spee*. She held it up against her chest like a locket, something pressed against the heart for luck: a pledge of allegiance. She was waiting for a boy she didn't know, someone she'd never even seen a photograph of, an English acquaintance of her daughter Ariel's. Ariel was on a junior semester abroad, and the boy was the brother of one of her Warwickshire dormmates. He was an auto mechanic in Surrey, and because he'd so badly wanted to come to the States, Ariel had told him that if he needed a place, he could stay with her parents in New Jersey. She had written ahead to inform them. "I told John Spee he could stay in Michael's old room, unless you are still using it as an 'office.' In which case he can stay in mine."

*Office* in quotation marks. Millie had once hoped to start a business in that room, something to do with recycling and other environmental projects. She had hoped to be hired on a consultant basis, but every time she approached a business or community organization they seemed confounded as to what they would consult her for. For a time Millie had filled the room with business cards and supplies and receipts for various expenses in case she ever filed a real tax form. Her daughter and her husband had rolled their eyes and looked, embarrassed, in the other direction.

"*Office.*" Ariel made her quotation marks as four quick slashes, not the careful sixes and nines Millie had been trained long ago to write. There was something a bit spoiled about Ariel, a quiet impudence, which troubled Millie. She had written back to her daughter, "Your father and I have no real objections, and certainly it will be nice to meet your friend. But you must check with us next time *before* you volunteer *our home.*" She had stressed *our home* with a kind of sternness that lingered regretlessly. "You mustn't take things for granted." It was costing them good money to send Ariel abroad. Millie herself had never been to England. Or anywhere, when you got right down to it. Once, as a child, she had been to Florida, but she remembered so little of it. Mostly just the glare of the sky, and some vague and shuddering colors.

People filed out from the Newark customs gate, released and weary, one of them a thin, red-haired boy of about twenty. He lit a cigarette, scanned the crowd, and then, spying Millie, headed toward her. He wore an old, fraying camel hair sports jacket, sneakers of blue, man-made suede, and a baseball cap, which said *Yankees*, an ersatz inscription.

"Are you Mrs. Keegan?" he asked, pronouncing it *Kaygan*.

"Um, yes, I am," Millie said, and blushed as if surprised. She let the sign, which with its crayoned and overblown message now seemed ludicrous, drop to her side. Her other hand she thrust out in greeting. She tried to smile warmly but wondered if she looked "fakey," something Ariel sometimes accused her of. "It's like you're doing everything from a magazine article," Ariel had said. "It's like you're trying to be happy out of a book." Millie owned several books about trying to be happy.

John shifted his cigarette into his other hand and shook Millie's. "John Spee," he said. He pronounced it *Spay*. His hand was big and bony, like a chicken claw.

"Well, I hope your flight was uneventful," said Millie.

"Oh, not really," said John. "Sat next to a bloke with stories about the Vietnam War and watched two movies about it. *The Deer Hunter* and, uh, I forget the other." He seemed apprehensive yet proud of himself for having arrived where he'd arrived.

"Do you have any more luggage than that? Is that all you have?"

" 'Zall I got!" he chirped, holding a small duffel bag and turning around just enough to let Millie see his U.S. Army knapsack.

"You don't want this sign, do you?" asked Millie. She creased it, folded it in quarters like a napkin, and shoved it into her own bag. Over the PA system a woman's voice was repeating, "Mr. Boone, Mr. Daniel Boone. Please pick up the courtesy line."

"Isn't that funny," said Millie.

On the drive home to Terracebrook, John Spee took out a pack of Johnny Parliaments and chain-smoked. He told Millie about his life in Surrey, his mates at the pub there, in a suburb called Worcester Park. "Never was much of a student," he said, "so there was no chance of me going to university." He spoke of the scarcity of work and of his "flash car," which he had sold to pay for the trip. He had worked six years as an auto mechanic, a job that he had quit to come here. "I may stay in the States a long time," he said. "I'm thinking of New York City. Wish I hadn't had to sell me flash car, though." He looked out at a souped-up Chevrolet zooming by them.

"Yes, that's too bad," said Millie. What should she say? On the car radio there was news of the garbage barge, and she turned it up to hear. It had been rejected by two states and two foreign countries, and was floating, homeless, toward Texas. "I used to have a kind of business," she explained to John. "It was in garbage and trash recycling. Nothing really came of it, though." The radio announcer was quoting something now.

*The wretched refuse of our teeming shores*, he was saying. *Yeah, yeah, yeah*, he was saying.

"Now I'm taking a college course through the mail," Millie said, then reddened. This had been her secret. Even Hane didn't know. "Don't tell my husband," she added quickly. "He doesn't know. He doesn't quite approve of my interest in business. He's a teacher. Religious studies at the junior college."

John gazed out at the snag of car dealerships and the fast-food shacks of Route 22. "Is he a vicar or something?" He inhaled his cigarette, holding the smoke in like a thought.

"Oh, no," said Millie. She sighed a little. Hane did go to church every Sunday. He was, she knew, a faithful man. She herself had stopped going regularly over a year ago. Now she went only once in a while, like a visit to an art museum, and it saddened Hane, but she just couldn't help it. "It's not my thing," she had said to her husband. It was a phrase she had heard Ariel use, and it seemed a good one, powerful with self-forgiveness, like Ariel herself.

"The traffic on this route is almost always heavy," said Millie. "But everyone drives very fast, so it doesn't slow you down."

John glanced sideways at her. "You look a little like Ariel," he said.

"Really?" said Millie brightly, for she had always thought her daughter too pretty to have come from Hane and her. Ariel had the bones and eyes of someone else, the daughter of royalty, or a movie star. Mitzi Gaynor's child. Or the Queen's. Ironically, it had been Michael, their eldest, who had seemed so clearly theirs.

"Oh, yes," said John. "You don't think so?"

USUALLY in spring Millie hurried guests immediately out into the backyard so that they could see her prize tulips—which really weren't hers at all but had belonged to the people who owned the house before them. The woman had purchased prize bulbs and planted them even into the edge of the next-door neighbor's yard. The yards were small, for sure, but the couple had been a young managerial type, and Millie had thought perhaps aggressive gardening went with such people.

Millie swung the car into the driveway and switched off the ignition. "I'll spare you the tulips for now," she said to John. "You probably would like to rest. With jet lag and all."

"Yeah," said John. He got out of the car and swung his duffel bag over his shoulder. He surveyed the identical lawns, still a pale, wintry ocher, and the small, boxy split-levels, their stingy porches fronting the entrances like goatees. He looked startled. *He thought we were going to be rich Americans*, thought Millie. "Are you tired?" she said aloud.

"Not so bad." He breathed deeply and started to perspire.

Millie went up the steps, took a key out from behind the black metal mailbox, and opened the door. "Our home is yours," she said, swinging her arms wide, showing him in.

John stepped in with a lit cigarette between his teeth, his eyes squinting from the smoke. He put his bag and knapsack down and looked about the living room. There were encyclopedias and ceramic figurines. There were some pictures of Ariel placed high on a shelf. Much of the furniture was shredded and old. There was a Bible and a *Time* magazine on the coffee table.

"Let me show you your room," said Millie, and she took him down a short corridor and opened the door on the right. "This was once my son's room," she said, "but he's—he's no longer with us." John nodded somberly. "He's not dead," Millie hastened to add, "he's just not with us." She cleared her throat— there was something in it, a scratch, a bruise of words. "He left home ten years ago, and we never heard from him again. The police said drugs." Millie shrugged. "Maybe it was drugs."

John was looking for a place to flick his ashes. Millie grabbed a potted begonia from the sill and held it out for him. "There's a desk and a filing cabinet here, which I was using for my business, so you can just ignore those." On the opposite wall there was a cot and a blond birch dresser. "Let me know if you need anything. Oh! Towels are in the bathroom, on the back of the door."

"Thanks," said John, and he looked at his watch like a man with plans.

"LEFTOVERS is all we've got tonight!" Millie emerged from the kitchen with quilted pot-holder mittens and a large cast-iron skillet. She beamed like the presenters on the awards shows she sometimes watched; she liked to watch TV when it was full of happiness.

Hane, who had met John coming out of the bathroom and had mumbled an embarrassed how-do-you-do, now sat at the head of the dining room table, waiting to serve the food. John sat kitty-corner, Michael's old place. He regarded the salad bowl, the clover outlines of the peppers, the clock stares of the tomato slices. He had taken a shower and parted his wet hair rather violently on the left.

"You'd think we'd be able to do a little better than this on your first night in America," said Hane, poking with a serving spoon at the fried pallet of mashed potatoes, turnips, chopped broccoli, and three eggs over easy. "Millie here, as you probably know already, is devoted to recycling." His tone was of good-natured mortification, a self-deprecating singsong that was his way of reprimanding his family. He made no real distinction between himself and his family. They were he. They were his feminine, sentimental side and warranted, even required, running commentary.

"It's all very fine," said John.

"Would you like skim milk or whole?" Millie asked him.

"Whole, I think," and then, in something of a fluster, he said, "Water, I mean, please. Don't trouble yourself, Mrs. Keegan."

"In New Jersey, water's as much trouble as milk," said Millie. "Have whichever you want, dear."

"Water, please, then."

"Are you sure?"

"Milk, then, I guess, thank you."

Millie went back into the kitchen to get milk. She wondered whether John thought they were poor and milk a little too expensive for them. The neighborhood probably did look shabby. Millie herself had been disappointed when they'd first moved here from the north part of town, after Ariel had started college and Hane had not been promoted to full professor rank, as he had hoped. It had been the only time she had ever seen her husband cry, and she had started to think of themselves as poor, though she knew that was silly. At least a little silly.

Millie stared into the refrigerator, not looking hungrily for something, anything, to assuage her restlessness, as she had when she was younger, but now forgetting altogether why she was there. *Look in the refrigerator*, was her husband's old joke about where to look for something she'd misplaced. "Places to look for your mind," he'd say, and then he'd recite a list. Once she had put a manila folder in the freezer by mistake.

"What did I want?" she said aloud, and the refrigerator motor kicked on in response to the warm air. She had held the door open too long. She closed it and went back and stood in the dining room for a moment. Seeing John's empty glass, she said, "Milk. That's right," and promptly went and got it.

"So how was the flight over?" asked Hane, handing John a plate of food. "If this is too much turnip, let me know. Just help yourself to salad." It had been years since they'd had a boy in the house, and he wondered if he knew how to talk to one. Or if he ever had. "Wait until they grow up," he had said to Millie of their own two children. "Then I'll know what to say to them." Even at student conferences he tended to ramble a bit, staring out the window, never, never into their eyes.

"By the time they've grown up it'll be too late," Millie had said.

But Hane had thought, *No, it won't.* By that time he would be president of the college, or dean of a theological school somewhere, and he would be speaking from a point of achievement that would mean something to his children. He could then tell them his life story. In the meantime, his kids hadn't seemed interested in his attempts at conversation. "Forget it, Dad," his son had always said to him. "Just forget it." No matter what Hane said, standing in a doorway or serving dinner—"How was school, son?"—Michael would always tell him just to forget it, Dad. One time, in the living room, Hane had found himself unable to bear it, and had grabbed Michael by the arm and struck him twice in the face.

"This is fine, thank you," said John, referring to his turnips. "And the flight was fine. I saw movies."

"Now, what is it you plan to do here exactly?" There was a gruffness in Hane's voice. This happened often, though Hane rarely intended it, or even heard it, clawing there in the punctuation.

John gulped at some milk and fussed with his napkin.

"Hane, let's save it for after grace," said Millie.

"Your turn," said Hane, and he nodded and bowed his head. John Spee sat upright and stared.

Millie began. " 'Bless this food to our use, and us to thy service. And keep us ever needful of the minds of others.' Wopes. 'Amen.' Did you hear what I said?" She grinned, as if pleased.

"We assumed you did that on purpose, didn't we, John?" Hane looked out over his glasses and smiled conspiratorially at the boy.

"Yes," said John. He looked at the ceramic figurines on the shelf to his right. There was a ballerina and a clown.

"Well," said Millie, "maybe I just did." She placed her

napkin in her lap and began eating. She enjoyed the leftovers, the warm, rising grease of them, their taste and ecology.

"It's very good food, Mrs. Keegan," said John, chewing.

"Before you leave, of course, I'll cook up a real meal. Several."

"How long you staying?" Hane asked.

Millie put her fork down. "Hane, I told you: three weeks."

"Maybe only two," said John Spee. The idea seemed to cheer him. "But then maybe I'll find a flat in the Big Apple and stay forever."

Millie nodded. People from out of town were always referring to the Big Apple, like some large forbidden fruit one conquered with mountain gear. It seemed to give them energy, to think of it that way.

"What will you *do*?" Hane studied the food on his fork, letting it hover there, between his fork and his mouth, a kind of ingestive purgatory. Hane's big fear was idleness. Particularly in boys. *What will you do?*

"Hane," cautioned Millie.

"In England none of me mates have jobs. They're all jealous 'cause I sold the car and came here to New York."

"This is New Jersey, dear," said Millie. "You'll see New York tomorrow. I'll give you a timetable for the train."

"You sold your car," repeated Hane. Hane had never once sold a car outright. He had always traded them in. "That's quite a step."

THE NEXT MORNING Millie made a list of things for John to do and see in New York. Hane had already left for his office. She sat at the dining room table and wrote:

*Statue of Liberty*
*World Trade Center*

*Times Square*
*Broadway 2-fors*

She stopped for a moment and thought.

*Metropolitan Museum of Art*
*Circle Line Tour*

The door of the "guest" room was still closed. Funny how it pleased her to have someone in that space, someone really using it. For too long she had just sat in there doodling on her business cards and thinking about Michael. The business cards had been made from recycled paper, but the printers had forgotten to mention that on the back. So she had inked it in herself. They had also forgotten to print Millie's middle initial— Environmental Project Adviser, Mildred *R.* Keegan—and so she had sat in there for weeks, ballpointing the *R* back in, card after card. Later Ariel had told her the cards looked stupid that way, and Millie had had to agree. She then spent days sitting at the desk, cutting the cards into gyres, triangles, curlicues, like a madness, like a business turned madness. She left them, absentmindedly, around the house, and Hane began to find them in odd places—on the kitchen counter, on the toilet tank. He turned to her one night in bed and said, "Millie, you're fifty-one. You don't have to have a career. Really, you don't," and she put her hands to her face and wept.

John Spee came out of his room. He was completely dressed, his bright hair parted neat as a crease, the white of his scalp startling as surgery.

"I've made a list of things you'll probably want to do," said Millie.

John sat down. "What's this?" He pointed to the Metropolitan Museum of Art. "I'm not that keen to go to museums.

We always went to the British Museum for school. My sister likes that kind of stuff, but not me."

"These are only suggestions," said Millie. She placed a muffin and a quartered orange in front of him.

John smiled appreciatively. He picked up a piece of orange, pressed it against his teeth, and sucked it to a damp, stringy mat.

"I can drive you to the station to catch the ten-o-two train, if you want to leave in fifteen minutes," said Millie. She slid sidesaddle into a chair and began eating a second muffin. Her manner was sprinkled with youthful motions, as if her body were on occasion falling into a memory or a wish.

"That would be lovely, thanks," said John.

"Did you really not like living in England?" asked Millie, but they were both eating muffins, and it was hard to talk.

At the station she pressed a twenty into his hand and kissed him on the cheek. He stepped back away from her and got on the train. "See a play," Millie mouthed at him through the window.

AT DINNER it was just she and Hane. Hane was talking about Jesus again, the Historical Jesus, how everyone misunderstood Christ's prophetic powers, how Jesus himself had been mistaken.

"Jesus thought the world was going to end," said Hane, "but he was wrong. It wasn't just Jerusalem. He was predicting the end for the whole world. Eschatologically, he got it wrong. He said it outright, but he was mistaken. The world kept right on."

"Perhaps he meant it as a kind of symbol. You know, poetically, not literally." Millie had heard Hane suggest this himself. They were his words she was speaking, one side of his own self-argument.

"No, he meant it literally," Hane barked a little fiercely.

"Well, we all make mistakes," said Millie. "Isn't the world

funny that way." She always tried to listen to Hane. She knew that few students registered for his courses anymore, and those that did tended to be local fundamentalists, young ignorant people, said Hane, who had no use for history or metaphor. They might as well just chuck the Bible! In class Hane's primary aim was reconciling religion with science and history, but these young "Pentecostalists," as Hane referred to them, didn't believe in science or history. "They're mindless, some of these kids. And if you want your soul nourished—and they do, I think—you've got to have a mind."

"Cleanliness is next to godliness," said Millie.

"What are you talking about?" asked Hane. He looked depressed and impatient. There were times when he felt he had married a stupid woman, and it made him feel alone in the world.

"I've been thinking about the garbage barge," said Millie. "I guess my mind's wandering around, just like that heap of trash." She smiled. She had been listening to all the reports on the barge, had charted its course from Islip, where she had relatives, to Morehead City, where she had relatives. "Imagine," she had said to her neighbor in their backyards, near the prize tulips that belonged to neither one of them. "Relatives in both places! Garbagey relatives!"

Millie wiped her mouth with her napkin. "It has nowhere to go," she said now to her husband.

Hane served himself more leftovers. He thought of Millie and this interest of hers in ecology. It baffled and awed him, like a female thing. In the kitchen Millie kept an assortment of boxes for recycling household supplies. She had boxes marked *Aluminum, Plastic, Dry Trash, Wet Trash, Garbage.* She had twice told him the difference between garbage and trash, but the distinction never meant that much to him, and he always forgot it. Last night she had told him about swans in the park who were making their nests from old boots and plastic six-pack rings. "Laying their eggs in litter," she'd said. Then she told him to be more fatherly toward John Spee, to take a friendly interest in the boy.

"Is this the end of the leftovers?" asked Hane. At his office at the college he ate very light lunches. Often he just brought a hard-boiled egg and sprinkled it carefully with salt, shaking the egg over the wastebasket if he got too much on by mistake.

"This is it," said Millie, standing. She picked up the skillet, and taking a serving spoon, scraped and swirled up the hardened, flat-bottomed remnants. "Here," she said, holding it all in front of Hane. "Open up."

Hane scowled. "Come on, Millie."

"Just one last spoonful. Tomorrow I cook fresh."

Hane opened his mouth, and Millie fed him gently, carefully, because the spoon was large.

Afterward they both sat in the living room and Hane read aloud a passage from 2 Thessalonians. Millie stared off like a child at the figurines, the clown and the ballerina, and thought about Ariel, traveling to foreign countries and meeting people. What it must be like to be young today, with all those opportunities. Once, last semester, before she'd left for England, Ariel had said, "You know, Mom, there's a girl in my class at Rutgers with exactly your name: Mildred Keegan. Spelled the same and everything."

"Really?" exclaimed Millie. Her face had lit up. This was interesting.

But Ariel was struck with afterthought. "Yeah. Only . . . well, actually she flunked out last week." Then Ariel began to laugh, and had to get up and leave the room.

AT NINE O'CLOCK, after she had peeled the labels off an assortment of tin cans, and rinsed and stacked them, Millie went to pick up John Spee at the train station.

"So what all did you do in the city?" asked Millie, slowing

for a red light and glancing at the boy. She had left the house in too much of a rush, and now, looking quickly in the rearview mirror, she attempted to smooth the front of her hair, which had fallen onto her forehead in a loose, droopy tangle. "Did you see a play? I hear there's some funny ones." Millie loved plays, but Hane didn't so much.

"No, didn't feel like buzzing the bees for a play." He said *ply*.

"Oh," said Millie. Her features sagged to a slight frown. Buzzing the bees. Ariel had used this expression once. *Money, honey, bees*, Ariel had explained impatiently. *Get it?* "Did you go down to Battery Park and see the Statue of Liberty? It's so beautiful since they cleaned it." Not that Millie had seen it herself, but it was in all the newsmagazines a while back, and the pictures had made it seem very holy and grand.

The light turned green, and she swung the car around the corner. At night this part of New Jersey could seem quiet and sweet as a real hometown.

"I just walked around and looked at the buildings," said John, glancing away from her, out the car window at the small darkened business district of Terracebrook. "I went to the top of the Empire State Building, and then I went back and went to the top again."

"You went twice."

"Twice, yeah. Twice."

"Well, good!" Millie exclaimed. And when they pulled into the driveway, she exclaimed it again. "Well, good!"

"SO HOW WAS the city?" boomed Hane, rising stiff and hearty, so awkwardly wanting to make the boy feel at home that he lunged at him a bit, big and creaky in the joints from having been sitting and reading all evening.

"Fine, thank you," said John, who then went quickly to his room.

Millie gave Hane a worried look, then followed and knocked on John's door. "John, would you like some supper? I've got a can of soup and some bread and cheese for a sandwich."

"No, thank you," John called through the door. Millie thought she heard him crying—was he crying? She walked back into the living room toward Hane, who gave her a shrug, helpless, bewildered. He looked at her for some reassuring word.

Millie shrugged back and walked past him into the kitchen. Hane followed her and stood in the doorway.

"I guess I'm not the right sort of person for him," he said. "I'm not a friendly man by nature. That's what he needs." Hane took off his glasses and cleaned them on the hem of his shirt.

"You're a stack of apologies," said Millie, kissing him on the cheek. "Here. Squash this can." She bent over and put a rinsed and label-less can near his shoe. Hane lifted his foot and came down on it with a bang.

THE NEXT MORNING was Friday, and John Spee wanted to go into the city again. Millie drove him to catch the ten-o-two. "Have a nice time," she said to him on the platform. "I'll pick you up tonight." As the train pulled up, steamy and deafening, she reminded him again about the half-price tickets for Broadway shows.

Back at the house, Millie got out the Hoover and began vacuuming. Hane, who had no classes on Friday, sat in the living room doing a crossword puzzle. Millie vacuumed around his feet. "Lift up," she said.

In John Spee's close and cluttered room she vacuumed the sills, even vacuumed the ceiling and the air, before she had to stop. All around the floor there were matchbooks from Greek coffee shops and odd fliers handed out on the street: *Live Eddie; Crazy Girls; 20% off Dinner Specials, now until Easter.* Underwear had been tossed on the floor, and there were socks balled in one corner of the desk.

Millie flicked off the Hoover and began to tidy the desktop. This was at one time to have been her business headquarters, and now look at it. She picked up the socks and noticed a spiral notebook underneath. It looked a little like a notebook she had been using for her correspondence course, the same shade of blue, and she opened it to see.

On the first page was written, *Crazy People I Have Met in America*. Underneath there was a list.

1. *Asian man in business suit waiting on subway platform. Screaming.*

2. *Woman in park walking dog. Screaming. Tells dog to walk like a lady.*

3. *In coffee shop, woman with food spilling out of her mouth. Yells at fork.*

Millie closed the notebook quickly. She was afraid to read on, afraid of what number four might be, or number five. She put the notebook out of her mind and moved away from the desk, unplugged the Hoover, wound up the cord, then collected the odd, inside-out clumps of clothes from under the cot and thought again of her garbage business, how she had hoped to run it out of this very room, how it seemed now to have crawled back in here—her poor little business!—looking a lot like laundry. What she had wanted was garbage, and instead she got laundry. "Ha!" She laughed out loud.

"What?" called Hane. He was still doing the crossword in the living room.

"Not you," said Millie. "I'm just going to put some things in the wash for John." She went downstairs to the laundry room, with its hampers of recyclable rags, its boxes of biodegradable detergent, its cartons of bottles with the labels soaked off them, the bags of aluminum foil and tins. *This* was an office, in a way, a one-woman room: a stand against the world. Or *for* the world. She meant *for* the world.

Millie flicked on the radio she kept propped on the dryer. She waited through two commercials, and then the news came on: The garbage barge was heading back from Louisiana. "I'll bet in that garbage there's a lot of trash," she wagered aloud. This was her distinction between garbage and trash, which she had explained many times to Hane: Garbage was moist and rotting and had to be plowed under. Trash was primmer and papery and could be reused. Garbage could be burned for gas, but trash could be dressed up and reissued. Retissued! Recycled Kleenex, made from cheap, recyclable paper—that was a truly viable thing, that was something she had hoped to emphasize, but perhaps she had not highlighted it enough in her initial materials. Perhaps people thought she was talking about garbage when she was talking about trash. Or vice versa. Perhaps no one had understood. Certainly, she had neglected to stress her best idea, the one about subliminal advertising on soap operas: having characters talk about their diseases and affairs at the same time that they peeled labels off cans and bundled newspapers. She was sure you could get programs to do this.

She turned the washer dial to *Gentle* and pushed it in. Warm water rushed into the machine like a falls, like a honeymoon, recycled, the same one, over and over.

WHEN MILLIE picked John up at the station, he told her about the buildings again.

"You probably didn't get a chance to see a play, then," said Millie, but he didn't seem to hear her.

"Going in tomorrow to look some more," he said. He flicked his lighter until it lit. He smoked nervously. "Great cars there, too."

"Well, wonderful," said Millie. But when she looked at

him there was a grayness in his face. His life seemed to be untacking itself, lying loose about him like a blouse. A life could do that. Millie thought of people in the neighborhood she might introduce him to. There was a boy of about twenty-two who lived down the street. He worked at a lawn and seed company and seemed like the friendly sort.

"There's someone on the street I should introduce you to," she said. "He's a boy about your age. I think you'd like him."

"Really don't want to meet anyone," he said. He pronounced it *mate*. "Unless I off to."

"Oh, no," said Millie. "You don't off to." Sometimes she slipped accidentally into his accent. She hoped it made him feel more at home.

In the morning she drove him again to the station for the ten-o-two train. "I'm getting fond of this little jaunt every day," she said. She smiled and meant it. She threw her arms around the boy, and this time he kissed her back.

AT MIDNIGHT that same day, Ariel phoned from Europe. She was traveling through the Continent—English universities had long spring vacations, a month, and she had headed off to France and to Italy, from where she was calling.

"Venice!" exclaimed Millie. "How wonderful!"

"That's just great, honey," said Hane on the bedroom extension. He didn't like to travel much, but he didn't mind it in other people.

"Of course," said Ariel, "there's an illusion here that you are separate from the garbage. That the water and food are different from the canal sewage. It's a crucial illusion to maintain. A psychological passport."

A psychological passport! How her daughter spoke! Children just got so far away from you. "What's the food like?" asked Millie. "Are you eating a lot of manicotti?"

"Swamp food. Watercress and dark fishes."

"Oh, I so envy you," said Millie. "Imagine, Hane, being in Venice, Italy."

"How's John Spee?" asked Ariel, changing the subject. Often when she phoned her parents, they each got on separate extensions and just talked to each other. They discussed money problems and the other's faults with a ferocity they couldn't quite manage face to face.

"All right," said Millie. "John is out taking a walk right now around the neighborhood, though it's a little late for it."

"He is? What time is it?"

"It's about midnight," said Hane on the other extension. He was in his pajamas, under the covers.

"Gee, I miscalculated the time. I hope I didn't wake you guys up."

"Of course not, honey," said Millie. "You can phone anytime."

"So it's midnight and John Spee's walking around in that depressing suburban neighborhood? How frightening." Ariel's voice was staticky but loud. The thoughtless singsong of her words sunk its way into Millie like something both rusty and honed. "Is he alone?"

"Yes," said Millie. "He probably just wanted some fresh air. He's been spending all his days in the city. He keeps going to the top of the Empire State Building, then just walks around looking at other tall buildings. And the cars. He hasn't been to any plays or anything."

There was a silence. Hane cleared his throat and said into the phone, "I suppose I'm not the best sort of person for him. He probably needs a man who is better with kids. Somebody athletic, maybe."

"Tell us more about Italy, dear," Millie broke in. She imagined Italy would be like Florida, all colors and light, but with a glorious ruin here and there, and large stone men with no clothes but with lovely pigeons on their heads. Perhaps there were plays.

"It's great," said Ariel. "It's hard to describe."

At twelve-fifteen they hung up. Hane, because he was reading the Scripture the next morning in church, went off to sleep. But Millie was restless and roamed the house, room after room, waiting for John to return. She thought about Ariel again, how much the girl's approval had come to mean to her, and wondered how one's children got so powerful that way. The week before Ariel left for England, the two of them had gone to a movie together. It was something they had not done since Ariel had been little, and so Millie had looked forward to it, like a kind of party. But during the opening credits Millie had started talking. She started to tell Ariel about someone she knew who used to be a garbage man but who was now making short industrial films for different companies. He had taken a correspondence course.

"Mom, you're talking so loudly," Ariel hissed at her in the dark of the movie theater. Ariel had pressed her index finger to her lips and said, "Shhhh!" as if Millie were a child. The movie had started, and Millie looked away, her face crumpling, her hand to her eyes so her daughter couldn't see. She tried to concentrate on the movie, the sounds and voices of it, but it all seemed underwater and far away. When afterward, in a restaurant, Ariel wanted to discuss the film, the way she said she always did—an *intellectual* discussion like a college course— Millie had just nodded and shrugged. Occasionally she had tried to smile at her daughter, saying, "Oh, I agree with you there," but the smile flickered and trembled and Ariel had looked at her, at a loss, as if her own mother were an idiot who had followed her to the movie theater, hoping only for a kind word or a dime.

Millie looked out the guest room window—John Spee's room—into the night to see whether she might spy John, circling the house or kicking a stone along the street. The moon was full, a porthole of sun, and Millie half expected to glimpse John sitting on someone's front step, not theirs, kneecaps pressed into the soft bulges of his eyes. How disappointing America must seem. To wander the streets of a city that was not yours, a city with its back turned, to be a boy from far away and step ashore here, one's imagination suddenly so concrete and mistaken, how could that not break your heart? But perhaps, she thought, John had dreamed so long and hard of this place that he had hoped it right out of existence. Probably no place in the world could withstand such an assault of human wishing.

She turned away from the window and again opened the blue notebook on the desk.

*More Crazy People I Have Seen in the States (than anywhere).*

*11. Woman with white worms on her legs. Flicking off worms.*

*12. Girl on library steps, the step is her home. Comb and mirror and toothbrush with something mashed in it laid out on step like a dressertop. No teeth. Screaming.*

*13. Stumbling man. Arms folded across his chest. Bumps into me hard. Bumps with hate in his eyes. I think, 'This bloke hates me, why does he hate me?' It smells. I run a little until I am away.*

The front door creaked open, and shut with a thud. Millie closed the notebook and went out into the living room in just her nightgown. She wanted to say good night and make certain John locked the door.

He seemed surprised to see her. "Thought I'd just hit the hay," he said. This was something he'd probably heard Ariel say once. It was something she liked to say.

"Ariel phoned while you were out," said Millie. She folded her arms across her breasts to hide them, in case they showed through her thin gown.

"That so?" John's face seemed to brighten and fall at the same time. He combed a hand through his hair, and strands dropped back across his part in a zigzag of orange. "She's coming home soon, is she?" It occurred to Millie that John didn't know Ariel well at all.

"No," she said. "She's traveling on the Continent. That's how Ariel says it: *on the Continent.* But she asked about you and says hello."

John looked away, hung up his coat in the front closet, on a hook next to his baseball cap, which he hadn't worn since his first day. "Thought she might be coming home," said John. He couldn't look directly at Millie. Something was sinking in him like a stone.

"Can I make you some warm milk?" asked Millie. She looked in the direction John seemed to be looking: at the photographs of Ariel. There she was at her high school graduation, all formal innocence, lies snapped and pretty. It seemed now to Millie that Ariel was too attractive, that she was careless and hurt people.

"I'll just go to bed, thanks," said John.

"I put your clean clothes at the foot of it, folded," said Millie.

"Thank you very much," he said, and he brushed past her, then apologized. "So sorry," he said, stepping away.

"Maybe we can all go into New York together next week," she blurted. She aimed it at his spine, hoping to fetch him back. He stopped and turned. "We can go out to eat," she continued. "And maybe take a tour of the UN." She'd seen picture postcards of the flags out front, rippling like sheets, all that international laundry, though she'd never actually been.

"OK," said John. He smiled. Then he turned back and

walked down the hall, trading one room for another, moving through and past, leaving Millie standing there, the way when, having decided anything, once and for all, you leave somebody behind.

IN THE MORNING there was just a note and a gift. "Thank you for lodging me. I decided early to take the bus to California. Please do not think me rude. Yours kindly, John Spee."

Millie let out a gasp of dismay. "Hane, the boy has gone!" Hane was dressing for church and came out to see. He was in a shirt and boxer shorts, and had been tying his tie. Now he stopped, as if some ghost that had once been cast from the house had just returned. The morning's Scripture was going to be taken from the third chapter of John, and parts of it were bouncing around in his head, like nonsense or a chant. *For God so loved the world* . . . John Spee was gone. Hane placed his hands on Millie's shoulders. What could he tell her? *For God so loved the world?* He didn't really believe that God loved the world, at least not in the way most people thought. *Love*, in this case, he felt, was a way of speaking. A *metaphor*. Though for what, he didn't exactly know.

"Oh, I hope he'll be OK," Millie said, and started to cry. She pulled her robe tight around her and placed one hand over her lips to hide their quivering. It was terrible to lose a boy. Girls could make their way all right, but boys went out into the world, limping with notions, and they never came back.

IT WAS A MONTH later when Millie and Hane heard from Ariel that John Spee had returned to England. He had taken the bus to Los Angeles, gotten out, walked around for a few hours, then had climbed back on and ridden six straight days back to Newark Airport. He had wanted to see San Francisco, but a man on the bus had told him not to go, that everyone was dying there. So John went to Los Angeles instead. For three hours. *Can you believe it?* wrote Ariel. She was back in War-wickshire, and John sometimes dropped by to see her when she was very, very busy.

The gift, when Millie unwrapped it, had turned out to be a toaster—a large one that could toast four slices at once. She had never seen John come into the house with a package, and she had no idea when or where he had gotten it.

"Four slices," she said to Hane, who never ate much bread. "What will we do with such a thing?"

Every night through that May and June, Millie curled against Hane, one of her hands on his hip, the smells of his skin all through her head. Summer tapped at the bedroom screens, nightsounds, and Millie would lie awake, not sleeping at all. "Oh!" she sometimes said aloud, though for no reason she could explain. Hane continued to talk about the Historical Jesus. Millie rubbed his shins while he spoke, her palm against the dry, whitening hair of him. Sometimes she talked about the garbage barge, which was now docked off Coney Island, a failed ride, an unamusement.

"Maybe," she said once to Hane, then stopped, her cheek against his shoulder. How familiar skin flickered in and out of strangeness; how it was yours no matter, no mere matter. "Maybe we can go someplace someday."

Hane shifted toward her, a bit plain and a bit handsome without his glasses. Through the window the streetlights shim-mered a pale green, and the moon shone woolly and bitten. Hane looked at his wife. She had the round, drying face of someone who once and briefly—a long ago fall, a weekend perhaps—had been very pretty without ever even knowing it. "You are my only friend," he said, and he kissed her, hard on the brow, like a sign for her to hold close.

# The Jewish Hunter

THIS WAS IN a faraway land. There were gyms but no irony or coffee shops. People took things literally, without drugs. Laird, who wanted to fix her up with this guy, warned her beforehand in exercise class. "Look, Odette, you're a poet. You've been in po biz for what—twenty years—"

"Only fifteen, I'm sure." She had just turned forty and scowled at him over her shoulder. She had a voice menopausal with whiskey, a voice left to lurch and ruin by cigarettes. It was without a middle range, low, with sudden cracks upward. "I hate that phrase *po biz*."

"Fifteen. All right. This guy's not at all literary. He's a farm lawyer. He gets the occasional flasher, or a Gypsy from the Serbo neighborhood in Chicago, but that's as artistic as he gets. He's dealing with farmers and farms. He wouldn't know T. S. Eliot from, say, *Pinky* Eliot. He's probably never even been to Minneapolis, let alone New York."

"Who's Pinky Eliot?" she asked. They were lying side by side, doing these things where you thrust your arms between your raised knees, to tighten the stomach muscles. There was loud music to distract you from worries that you might not know anyone in the room well enough to be doing this in front of them. "Who the heck is Pinky Eliot?"

"Someone I went to fourth grade with," said Laird, gasping.

"It was said he weighed more than the teacher, and she was no zipper, let me tell you." Laird was balding, and in exercise class the blood rushed across his head, bits of hair curling above his ears like gift ribbon. He had lived in this town until he was ten, then his family had moved east to New Jersey, where she had first met him, years ago. Now he had come back, like a salmon, to raise his own kids. He and his wife had two. "Little and Moist," they called them. "Look, you're in the boonies here. You got your Pinky Eliot or you got your guy who's never heard of Pinky or any Eliot."

She had been in the boonies before. To afford her apartment in New York, she often took these sorts of library fellowships: six weeks and four thousand dollars to live in town, write unpublishable poems, and give a reading at the library. The problem with the boonies was that nobody ever kissed you there. They stared at you, up, down, but they never kissed.

Actually, once in a while you could get them to kiss.

But then you had to leave. And in your packing and going, in tearing the seams, the hems, the haws, you felt like some bad combination of Odysseus *and* Penelope. You felt funny in the heart.

"All right," she said. "What is his name?"

Laird sighed. "Pinky Eliot," he said, thrusting his arms between his knees. "Somehow in this mangled presentation, I fear I've confused you."

PINKY ELIOT had lost weight, though for sure he still weighed more than the teacher. He was about forty-five, with all his hair still dark. He was not bad-looking, elf-nosed and cat-eyed, though a little soccer ball–ish through the chin and cheeks, which together formed a white sphere with a sudden scar curling grayly around. Also, he had the kind of mustache a college roommate of hers used to say looked like it had crawled up to find a warm spot to die.

They ate dinner at the only Italian restaurant in town. She drank two glasses of wine, the cool heat of it spreading through her like wintergreen. One of these days, she knew, she would have to give up dating. She had practiced declarations in the mirror. "I don't date. I'm sorry. I just don't date."

"I always kind of liked the food here," said Pinky.

She looked at his round face and felt a little bad for him and a little bad for herself while she was at it, because, truly, the food was not good: flavorless bladders of pasta passing as tortellini; the cutlets mealy and drenched in the kind of tomato sauce that was unwittingly, defeatedly orange. Poor Pinky didn't know a garlic from a Gumby.

"Yes," she said, trying to be charming. "But do you think it's really Italian? It feels as if it got as far as the Canary Islands, then fell into the water."

"An East Coast snob." He smiled. His voice was slow with prairie, thick with Great Lakes. "Dressed all in black and hating the Midwest. Are you Jewish?"

She bristled. A Nazi. A hillbilly Nazi gastronomical moron. "No, I'm not Jewish," she said archly, staring him down, to teach him, to teach him this: "Are *you?*"

"Yes," he said. He studied her eyes.

"Oh," she said.

"Not many of us in this part of the world, so I thought I'd ask."

"Yes." She felt an embarrassed sense of loss, as if something that should have been hers but wasn't had been taken away, legally, by the police. Her gaze dropped to her hands, which had started to move around nervously, independently, like small rodents kept as pets. Wine settled hotly in her cheeks, and when she rushed more to her mouth, the edge of the glass clinked against the tooth in front that was longer than all the others.

Pinky reached across the table and touched her hair. She

had had it permed into waves like ramen noodles the week before. "A little ethnic kink is always good to see," he said. "What are you, Methodist?"

ON THEIR SECOND DATE they went to a movie. It was about creatures from outer space who burrow into earthlings and force them to charge up enormous sums on their credit cards. It was an elaborate urban allegory, full of disease and despair, and Odette wanted to talk about it. "Pretty entertaining movie," said Pinky slowly. He had fidgeted in his seat through the whole thing and had twice gotten up and gone to the water fountain. "Just going to the bubbler," he'd whispered.

Now he wanted to go dancing.

"Where is there to go dancing?" said Odette. She was still thinking about the part where the two main characters had traded boom boxes and it had caused them to fall in love. She wanted either Pinky or herself to say something incisive or provocative about directorial vision, or the narrative parameters of cinematic imagery. But it looked as if neither of them was going to.

"There's a place out past the county beltline about six miles." They walked out into the parking lot, and he leaned over and kissed her cheek—intimate, premature, a leftover gesture from a recent love affair, no doubt—and she blushed. She was bad at love. There were people in the world who were good at love and people who were bad at it. She was bad. She used to think she was good at love, that it was intimacy she was bad at. But you had to have both. Love without intimacy, she knew, was an unsung tune. It was all in your head. You said, "Listen to this!" but what you found yourself singing was a tangle, a nothing, a heap. It reminded her of a dinner party she had gone to once, where dessert was served on plates printed with French songs. After dinner everyone had had to sing their plate, but hers had still had whipped cream on it, and when it came her turn, she had garbled the notes and words, frantically pushing the whipped cream around with a fork so she could see the next measure. Oh, she was bad, bad like that, at love.

Pinky drove them six miles south of the county beltline to a place called Humphrey Bogart's. It was rough and wooden, high-beamed, a former hunting lodge. On a makeshift stage at the front, a country-western band was playing "Tequila Sunrise" fifteen years too late, or perhaps too soon. Who could predict? Pinky took her hand and improvised a slow jitterbug to the bass. "What do I do now?" Odette kept calling to Pinky over the music. "What do I do now?"

"This," said Pinky. He had the former fat person's careful grace, and his hand at the small of her back felt big and light. His scar seemed to disappear in the dancelight, and his smile drove his mustache up into flattering shadow. Odette had always been thin and tense.

"We don't dance much in New York," she said.

"No? What do you do?"

"We, uh, just wait in line at cash machines."

Pinky leaned into her, took her hand tightly to his shoulder, and rocked. He put his mouth to her ear. "You've got a great personality," he said.


ON SUNDAY AFTERNOON Pinky took her to the Cave of the Many Mounds. "You'll like this," he said.

"Wonderful!" she said, getting into his car. There was a kind of local enthusiasm about things, which she was trying to get the hang of. It involved good posture and utterances made in a chirpy singsong. *Isn't the air just snappy?* She was wearing sunglasses and an oversize sweater. "I was thinking of asking you what a Cave of Many Mounds was, and then I said, 'Odette, do you *really* want to know?' " She fished through her pocketbook. "I mean, it sounds like a whorehouse. You don't happen to have any cigarettes, do you?"

Pinky tapped on her sunglasses. "You're not going to need these. It's dark in the cave." He started the car and pulled out.

"Well, let me know when we get there." She stared straight ahead. "I take it you don't have any cigarettes."

"No," said Pinky. "You smoke cigarettes?"

"Once in a while." They drove past two cars in a row with bleeding deer strapped on them like wreaths, like trophies, *like women*, she thought. "Damn hunters," she murmured.

"What kind of cigarettes do you smoke? Do you smoke Virginia Slims?" asked Pinky with a grin.

Odette turned and lowered her sunglasses, looked out over them at Pinky's sun-pale profile. "No, I don't smoke *Virginia Slims*."

"I'll bet you do. I'll bet you smoke Virginia Slims."

"Yeah, I smoke Virginia Slims," said Odette, shaking her head. Who was this guy?

Ten miles south, there started to be signs for Cave of the Many Mounds. CAVE OF THE MANY MOUNDS 20 MILES. CAVE OF THE MANY MOUNDS 15 MILES. At 5 MILES, Pinky pulled the car over onto the shoulder. There were only trees and in the far distance a barn and a lone cow.

"What are we doing?" asked Odette.

Pinky shifted the car into park but left the engine running. "I want to kiss you now, before we get in the cave and I lose complete control." He turned toward her, and suddenly his body, jacketed and huge, appeared suspended above her, hovering, as she sank back against the car door. He closed his eyes and kissed her, long and slow, and she left her sunglasses on so she could keep her eyes open and watch, see how his lashes closed on one another like petals, how his scar zoomed quiet and white about his cheek and chin, how his lips pushed sleepily against her own to find a nest in hers and to stay there, moving, as if in words, but then not in words at all, his hands going round her in a soft rustle, up the back of her sweater to her bare waist and spine, and spreading there, blooming large and holding her just briefly until he pulled away, gathered himself back to himself, and quietly shifted the car into drive.

Odette sat up and stared out the windshield into space. Pinky moved the car back out onto the highway and picked up speed.

"We don't do that in New York," rasped Odette. She cleared her throat.

"No?" Pinky smiled and put his hand on her thigh.

"No, it's, um, the cash machines. You just . . . you wait at them. Forever. Your whole life you're just always"—her hand sliced the air—"there."

"PLEASE DO NOT touch the formations," the cave tour guide kept shouting over everyone's head. Along the damp path through the cave there were lights, which allowed you to see walls marbled a golden rose, like a port cheddar; nippled projections, blind galleries, arteries all through the place, chalky and damp; stalagmites and stalactites in walrusy verticals, bursting up from the floor in yearning or hanging wicklessly in drips from the ceiling, making their way, through time, to the floor. The whole cave was in a weep, everything wet and slippery; still ocher pools of water bordered the walk, which spiraled gradually down. "Nature's Guggenheim," said Odette, and because Pinky seemed not to know what she was talking about, she said, "That's an art museum in New York." She had her sunglasses perched high on her head. She looked at Pinky gleefully, and he smiled back at her as if he thought she was cute but from outer space, like something that would soon be made into a major motion picture and then later into a toy.

". . . The way you can remember which are which," the guide was saying, "is to remember: When the mites go up, the tights come down . . ."

"Get that?" said Pinky too loudly, nudging her. "The tights come down?" People turned to look.

"What are you, hard of hearing?" asked Odette.

"A little," said Pinky. "In the right ear."

"Next we come to a stalagmite which is the only one in the cave that visitors are allowed to touch. As we pass, it will be on your right, and you may manhandle it to your heart's content."

"Hmmmph," said Pinky.

"Really," said Odette. She peered ahead at the front of the group, which had now gathered unexcitedly around the stalagmite, a short stumpy one with a head rubbed white with so much touching. It had all the appeal of a bar of soap in a gas station. "I think I want to go back and look at the cave coral again."

"Which was that?" said Pinky.

"All that stuff that looked like cement broccoli. Also the chapel room with the church organ. I mean, I thought that looked pretty much like an organ."

". . . And now," the guide was saying, "we come to that part of our tour when we let you see what the cave looks like in its own natural lighting." She moved over and flicked a switch. "You should not be able to see your hand in front of your face."

Odette widened her eyes and then squinted and still could not see her hand in front of her face. The darkness was thick and certain, not a shaded, waltzing dark but a paralyzing coffin jet. There was something fierce and eternal about it, something secret and unrelieved, like a thing not told to children.

"I'm right here," Pinky said, stepping close, "in case you need me." He gave her far shoulder a squeeze, his arm around the back of her. She could smell the soupy breath of him, the spice of his neck near her face, and leaned, blind and hungry, into his arm. She reached past the scratch of her own sweater and felt for his hand.

"We can see now how the cave looked when it was first unearthed, and how it had existed eons before, in the pitch dark, gradually growing larger, opening up in darkness, the life and the sea of it trapped and never seeing light, a small moist cavern a million years in the making, just slowly opening, opening, and opening inside. . . ."

WHEN THEY SLEPT TOGETHER, she almost cried. He was a kisser, and he kissed and kissed. It seemed the kindest thing that had ever happened to her. He kissed and whispered and brought her a large glass of water when she asked for one.

"When ya going back to New York?" he asked, and because it was in less than four weeks, she said, "Oh, I forget."

Pinky got out of bed. He was naked and unselfconscious, beautiful, in a way, the long, rounded lines of him, the stark cliff of his back. He went over to the VCR, fumbled with some cassettes in the dark, holding each up to the window, where there was a rainy, moony light from the street, like a dream; he picked up cassette after cassette until he found the one he wanted.

It was a tape called *Holocaust Survivors*, and the title flashed blood red on the television screen, as if in warning that it had no place there at all. "I watch this all the time," said Pinky, very quietly. He stared straight ahead in a trance of impassivity, but when he reached back to put an arm around Odette, he knew exactly where she was, slightly behind one of his shoulders, the sheet tight across her chest. "You shouldn't hide your breasts," he said, without looking. But she stayed like that, tucked close, all along the tracks to Treblinka, the gates to Auschwitz, the film lingering on weeds and wind, so unbelieving in this historical badlands, it seemed to want, in a wave of nausea and regret, to become perhaps a nature documentary.

It seemed at moments confused about what it was about, a confusion brought on by knowing exactly.

Someone was talking about the trucks. How they put people in trucks, with the exhaust pipes venting in, how they drove them around until they were blue, the people were blue, and could be shoveled out from a trapdoor. Past some barbed wire, asters were drying in a field.

When it was over, Pinky turned to her and sighed. "Heavy stuff," he said.

*Heavy stuff?* Her breathing stopped, then sped up, then stopped again. *Who on earth was entitled to such words?*

*Who on earth?* She felt, in every way it was possible to feel it, astonished that she had slept with him.

SHE WENT OUT with him again, but this time she greeted him at his own door, with a stiff smile and a handshake, like a woman willing to settle out of court. "So casual," he said, standing in the doorway. "I don't know. You East Coast city slickers."

"We got hard hearts," she said with an accent that wasn't really any particular accent at all. She wasn't good at accents.

When they slept together again, she tried not to make too much of it. Once more they watched *Holocaust Survivors*, a different tape, out of sequence, the camera still searching hard for something natural to gaze upon, embarrassed, like a bloodshot eye weary and afraid of people and what they do. *They set fire to the bodies and to the barracks*, said a voice. *The pyres burned for many days.*

Waves lapped. Rain beaded on a bulrush. In the bathroom she ran the tap water so he couldn't hear as she sat, ill, staring at her legs, her mother's legs. When had she gotten her mother's legs? When she crept back to his bed, he was sleeping like a boy, the way men did.

In the morning she got up early and went to the closest

thing there was to a deli and returned triumphantly with bagels and lox. Outside, the town had been museum dead, but the sky was lemony with sun, and elongations of light, ovals of brightened blue, now dappled Pinky's covers. She laid the breakfast out in them, and he rolled over and kissed her, his face waxy with sleep. He pointed at the lox. "You like that sort of stuff?"

"Yup." Her mouth was already full with it, the cool, slimy pink. "Eat it all the time."

He sighed and sank back into his pillow. "After breakfast I'll teach you some Yiddish words."

"I already know some Yiddish words. I'm from New York. Here, eat some of this."

"I'll teach you *tush* and *shmuck.*" Pinky yawned, then grinned. "And *shiksa.*"

"All the things a nice Jewish boy practices on before he marries a nice Jewish girl. I know those."

"What's wrong with you?"

She refused to look at him. "I don't know."

"*I* know," said Pinky, and he stood up on the bed, like a child about to bounce, toweringly naked, priapic. She could barely look. Oh, for a beaded bulrush. A train disappearing into a tunnel. "You're falling in love with me!" he exclaimed, gazing merrily down. She still had her coat on, and had stopped chewing. She stared, disbelievingly, up at him. Sometimes she thought she was just trying to have fun in life, and other times she realized she must be terribly confused. She narrowed her eyes. Then she opened her mouth wide so that he could see the train wreck of chewed-up bagel and lox.

"I like that," said Pinky. "You're onto something there."

HER POEMS, as she stated in letters to friends in New York, were not going well; she had put them on the back burner, and they had fallen behind the stove. She had met this guy. Something had happened to the two of them in a cave, she wasn't sure what. She had to get out of here. She was giving her final reading to the library patrons and matrons in less than three weeks, and that would pretty much be it. *I hope you are not wearing those new, puffy evening dresses I see in magazines. They make everyone look like sticky buns. It is cold. Love, Odette.*

LAIRD WAS CURIOUS. He kept turning his head sideways during the sit-ups. "So you and Pinky hitting it off?"

"Who knows?" said Odette.

"Well, I mean, everyone's had their difficulties in life; his I'm only a little aware of. I thought you'd find him interesting."

"Sure, anthropologically."

"You think he's a dork."

"Laird, we're in our forties here. You can't use words like *dork* anymore." The sit-ups were getting harder. "He's not a dork. He's a doofus. Maybe. Maybe a *doink*."

"You're a hard woman," said Laird.

"Oh, I'm not," pleaded Odette, collapsing on the rubber mat. "Really I'm not."

AT NIGHT he began to hold her in a way that stirred her deeply. He slept with one hand against the small of her back, the other capped against her head, as if to protect her from bad thoughts. Or, perhaps, thoughts at all. How quickly bodies came to love each other, promise themselves to each other always, without asking permission. From the mind! If only she could give up her mind, let her heart swell, inflamed, her brain stepping out for whole days, whole seasons, her work shrinking to limericks. She would open her mouth before the library fellowship people, and out would come: *There once was a woman from* . . . Someone would rush to a phone booth and call the police.

But perhaps you *could* live only from the neck down. Perhaps you *could* live with the clothes you were taking off all piled on top of your head, in front of your face, not just a sweater with a too-small neck but everything caught there—pants, shoes, and socks—a crazed tangle on your shoulders, in lieu of a head, while your body, stark naked, prepared to live the rest of its life in the sticks, the boonies, the fly-over, the rain. Perhaps you could. For when she slept against him like that, all the rest of the world collapsed into a suitcase under the bed. It was the end of desire, this having. Oh, here oh here she was. He would wrap himself around her, take her head like an infant's into his hand and breathe things to her, her throat her chest, in his beginning to sleep. *Go to sleep, go to sleep with me.*

IN THE MORNING she warmed her arms over the blue zinnias of the gas jets and heated water for coffee and eggs. Over the newspaper, she pretended she and Pinky were Beatrice and Benedick, or Nick and Nora Charles, which is what she always pretended in a love affair, at least for a few days, until the evidence overwhelmed her.

"Why are you always talking with your hands?" asked Pinky. "You think you're Jewish?"

She glared at him. "You know, that's what I hate about this part of the country," she replied. "Everyone's so repressed. If you use your body in the least way while you're talking, people think you're trying out for a Broadway show."

"Kiss me," he said, and he closed his eyes.

On a weekday Pinky would be off to his office, to work on another farm bankruptcy or a case of animal abuse. "My clients," he said wearily. "You would never want to go out to eat with them. They come into my office reeking of cowshit, they lean back in the chair, set their belly out like that, then tell you about how some Humane Society bastard gave them a summons because their goat had worms." Across his face there breathed a sigh of tragedy. "It's a sad thing not to have clients you can go out to eat with." He shook his head. "It's a sad thing, a goat with worms."

There was something nice about Pinky, but that something was not Nick Charles. Pinky was more like a grave and serious brother of Nick's, named Chuck. Chuck Charles. When you had parents who would give you a name like that, there was nothing funny anymore.

"What do you write poems about?" he asked her once in the middle of the night.

"Whores," she said.

"Whores," he repeated, nodding in the dark.

She gave him books of poetry: Wordsworth, Whitman, all the W's. When she'd ask him how he liked them, he would say, "Fine. I'm on page . . ." and then he would tell her what page he was on and how many pages he'd accomplished that day. "The Wadsworth is a little too literaturey for me."

"Wordsworth," she corrected. They were in his kitchen, drinking juice.

"Wordsworth. Isn't there a poet named Wadsworth?"

"No. You're probably thinking of Longfellow. That was his middle name."

"Longfellow. Now who's he again?"

"How about *Leaves of Grass*? What did you think of the poems in there?"

"OK. I'm on page fifty," he said. Then he showed her his gun, which he kept in his kitchen in a leather case, like a trombone. He kept a rifle, he said, in the basement.

Odette frowned. "You hunt?"

"Sure. Jews aren't supposed to hunt, I know. But in this part of the country it's best to have a gun." He smiled. "*Bavarians*, you know. Here, try it out. Let me see how you look with a gun."

"I'm afraid of guns."

"Nothing to be afraid of. Just heft it and look down the top of the barrel and line up the sights."

She sighed, lifted the gun, pressed the butt hard against her right shoulder, and aimed it at the kitchen counter. "Now, see the notch in the metal sticking up in the middle of your barrel?" Pinky was saying. "You have to get the bead in the middle of the notch."

She closed her left eye. "I can feel the urge coming on to blow away that cutting board," she said.

"Gun's not loaded. Probably not till spring. Turkey season. Though I've got tags for deer."

"You hunt turkeys?" She put the gun down. It was heavy.

"You eat turkey, don't you?"

"The turkeys I eat are raised on farms. They're different. They've signed on the dotted line." She paused and sighed again. "What do you do, go into a field and fire away?"

"Kind of. You try to catch them midflight. You know, I should take you deer hunting. It's the last two days, this weekend, and I've got tags. Have you ever been?"

"*Pulease*," she said.

IT WAS COLD in the woods. She blew breath clouds, then rings of cigarette smoke, into the dead ferns. "It's nice out here. You don't suppose we could just watch nature instead of shoot it."

"Without hunting, the deer would starve," said Pinky.

"So maybe we could just cook for them." They had brought along a bottle of Jim Beam, and she twisted it open and took a swig. "Have you ever been married?"

"Once," said Pinky. "God, what, twenty years ago." He quickly shouldered his rifle, thinking he heard something, but no.

"Oh," she said. "I wasn't going to ask, but then you never said anything about it, so I thought I'd ask."

"How about you?"

"Not me," said Odette. She had a poem about marriage. It began, *Marriage is the death you want to die*, and in front of audiences she never read it with much conviction. Usually she swung her foot back and forth through the whole thing.

She looked down at her chest. "I don't think orange is anyone's most flattering color," she said. They were wearing blaze-orange hats and vests. "I think we look like things placed in the middle of the road to make the cars go around."

"Shhhh," said Pinky.

She took another swig of Jim Beam. She had worn the wrong kind of boots—gray, suede, over the knees, with three-inch heels—and now she studied them with interest. One of the heels was loose, and mud was drying on the toes. "Tell me again," she whispered to Pinky, "what makes us think a deer will cross our path?"

"There's a doe bed not far from here," whispered Pinky. "It attracts bucks."

"Bucks, doe—thank God everything boils down to money, I always say."

"During mating season the doe constructs a bed for herself, and then she urinates all around the outside of it. That's how she gets her mate."

"So *that's* it," murmured Odette. "I was always peeing *in* the bed."

Pinky's gun suddenly fired into the trees, and the noise filled the woods like a war, spilling to the ground the yellowing needles of a larch.

"Ahhhhhh!" Odette screamed. "What is going on?" Guns, she was reminded then, were not for girls. They were for boys. They were invented by boys. They were invented by boys who had never gotten over their disappointment that accompanying their own orgasm there wasn't a big *boom* sound. "What the hell are you doing?"

"Damn!" shouted Pinky. "I missed!" He stood up and went crashing through the underbrush.

"Oh, my God!" cried Odette, and she stumbled after him, snapping the same twigs underfoot, ducking the same barbed wire. "Where are we going?"

"I've only wounded the deer," Pinky called over his shoulder. "I've got to kill it."

"Do you have to?"

"Keep your voice down," said Pinky.

"Fuck you," said Odette. "I'll wait for you back where we were," but there was a sudden darting from a bush behind her, and the bleeding deer leaped out, in a mournful gallop, its hip a crimson gash. Pinky raised his gun and fired, catching the deer in the neck. The air shimmered in the echo, and the leaves fell from a horse chestnut. The deer's legs buckled, and when it tipped over, dead in some berry bushes, its eyes never blinked but stayed lidless and deep, black as outer space.

"I'll leave the entrails for the hawks," Pinky said to Odette, but she was not there.

.  .  .

>Oh, the ladies come down from the Pepsi Hotel
>Their home has no other name
>than the sign that was placed
>like a big cola bell: Pepsi-Cola Have a Pepsi Hotel.

Only a few of Odette's poems about whores rhymed—the ones she'd written recently—but perhaps the library crowd would like those best, the anticipation of it, knowing what the next word would be *like* though not what it would *be*; stanza after stanza, it would be a combination of comfort and surprise an audience might appreciate.

The local library association had set up a lectern near the windows of the reference room and had arranged chairs in rows for about eighty people. The room was chilly and alarmingly full. When Odette read she tried to look out past the faces, toward the atlases and the biographical dictionaries. She tugged on the cowl of her sweater and pulled it up over her chin between poems. She tried to pretend people's heads were all little ears of corn, something a dance instructor had once told her ballet class to do when she was seven and they had had to dance before the parents.

> *They come down to the truckers*
> *or the truckers go up*
> *to the rooms with the curtains pell-mell.*
> *They truck down for the fuckers*
> *or else they fuck up*
> *in the Pepsi Have a Pepsi Hotel.*

There was silence. A door creaked open then shut. Odette looked up and saw Pinky in the back, tiptoeing over to a chair to sit. She had not seen or spoken to him in a week. Two elderly women in the front turned around to stare.

> *Oh, honey, they sigh; oh, honey, they say,*
> *there are small things to give and to sell,*
> *and Heaven's among us*
> *so work can be play at the . . .*

There were other stanzas, too many, and she sped through them. She took a sip of water and read a poem called "Sleeping Wrong." *She slept wrong on her back last night*, it began, *and so she holds her head this way, mad with loneliness, madder still with talk.* She then read another long one, titled "Girl Gets Diphtheria, Loses Looks." She looked up and out. The audience was squinting back at her, their blood sugar levels low from early suppers, their interest redirected now and then toward her shoes,

which were pointy and beige. "I'll close," she said loudly into
the mike, "with a poem called 'Le Cirque in the Rain.' "

> *This is not about a french monkey circus*
> *discouraged by weather.*
> *This is about the restaurant*
> *you pull up to in a cab,*
> *your life stopping there and badly,*
> *like a dog's song,*
> *your heart put in funny.*

It told the story of a Manhattan call girl worrying a crisis of
faith. *What is a halo but a handsome accident / of light and orbiting
dust. What is a heart / but a . . .* She looked out at the two
elderly women sitting polite and half attentive, unfazed, in the
front row. One of them had gotten out some knitting. Odette
looked back at her page. *Chimp in the chest*, she had written in
an earlier draft, and that was what she said now.

Afterward a small reception was held out by the card cat-
alogs. There were little cubes of pepper cheese, like dice, placed
upon a table. There was a checkerboard of crackers, dark and
light, a roulette of cold cuts. "It's a goddamn casino." She
turned and spoke to Pinky, who had come up and put his arm
around her.

"I've missed you," he said. "I've been eating venison and
thinking of you."

"Yes, well, thank you for coming, anyway."

"I thought you read very well," he said. "Not all of it I
understood, I have to admit. Some of your stuff is a little too
literaturey for me."

"Really," said Odette.

People shook her hand. They looked at her quizzically, came
at her with assumptions, presumptions, what they believed was

intimate knowledge of her. She felt unarmed, by comparison; disadvantaged. She lit up a cigarette.

"Do you really feel that way about men?" asked a man with a skeptical mouth.

"Do you really feel that way about women?" asked someone else.

"Your voice," said a young student. "It's like—who's that actress?"

"Mercedes McCambridge," said her friend.

"No, not her. Oh, I forget."

Several elderly couples had put on their coats and hats, but they came up to Odette to shake her hand. "You were wonderful, dear," said one of the women, gazing into Odette's nose.

"Yes," said the other, studying her own botched knitting— a scarf with an undulating edge.

"We come to these every year," said a man standing next to her. He had been searching for something to say and had come up with this.

"Well, thank you for coming this year as well," said Odette, stupidly, and dragged on her cigarette.

Kay Stevens, the woman in charge of the fellowship readings, came up and kissed her on the cheek, the sweet vanilla wax of her lipstick sticking like candy. "A big success," she said quickly, and then frowned and hurried off.

"Can I buy you a drink somewhere?" asked Pinky. He was still standing beside her, and she turned to look at him gratefully.

"Oy," she said. "Please."

Pinky drove them out past the county line to Humphrey Bogart's. He toasted her, flicked a sparkly speck of something from her cheek, looked into her eyes, and said, "Congratulations." He grew drunk, pulled his chair close, and put his head on her shoulder. He listened to the music, chewed on his cocktail straw, tapped his feet.

"Any requests?" the bandleader rumbled into the mike.

"O, give us one of the songs of Zion," shouted Pinky.

"What was that?" The words popped and roared in the mike.

"Nothing," said Pinky.

"Maybe we should go," said Odette, reaching for Pinky's hand beneath the table.

"OK," he said. "All right."

HE STRUCK a match to a candle in the dark of his bedroom, and the fire of it lit the wall in a jittery paint. He came back to her and pressed close. "Why don't I go with you to New York?" he whispered. She was silent, and so he said, "No, I think you should stay here. I could take you cross-country skiing."

"I don't like cross-country skiing," she whispered back. "It reminds me of when you're little and you put on your father's slippers and shluff around the house like that."

"I could take you snowmobiling up by Sand Lake." There was another long silence. Pinky sighed. "No, you won't. I can see you phoning your friends back East to tell them you'd decided to stay and them shrieking, 'You did *what?*' "

"You know us East Coasters," she said desperately. "We just come into a place, rape and pillage."

"You know," said Pinky, "I think you are probably the smartest person I have ever known."

She stopped breathing. "You don't get out much, do you?"

He rolled back and stared at the shadowed ceiling, its dimples and blotches. "When I was in high school, I was a bad student. I had to take special classes in this house behind the school. It was called The House."

She rubbed his leg gently with her foot. "Are you trying to make me cry?"

He took her hand, brought it out from beneath the covers,

up to his mouth, and kissed it. "Everything's a joke with you,"
he said.

"Nothing's a joke with me. It just all comes out like one."

THEY SPENT one last night together. At his house, late, with
all the lights off, they watched another cassette of *Holocaust
Survivors*. It was about a boy forced to sing for the Nazis, over
and over. Because he could sing, he was the last to be shot in
the head, and when they shot him they missed the center of
his brain. He was found alive. "I must think of happy things,"
he said now, old and staring off. "It may not be what others
do, but it is what I must do." *He had a beautiful voice*, said a
woman, another survivor. *It was beautiful like a bird that was
also a god with flutes.*

"Heavy," murmured Pinky, when it was over. He pressed
the remote control and turned away in the darkness, toward the
wall, in a curve of covers. Odette pulled herself close, placed
her hands around to the front of him, palms over the slight
mounds of his breasts, her fingers deep in the light tangle of
hair.

"Are you OK?" she asked.

He twisted toward her and kissed her, and in the dark he
seemed to her aged and sad. He placed one of her fingers to his
face. "You never asked about this." He guided her finger along
his chin and cheek, letting it dead-end, like the scar, in his
mustache.

"I try not to ask too many things. Once I start I can't stop."

"You want to know?"

"All right."

"I was in high school. Some guy called me a Jew, and I
went after him. But I was clumsy and fat. He broke a bottle
and dragged it across my face. I went home and my grandmother
nearly fainted. Funny thing was, I had no idea that I *was* Jewish.
My grandmother waited until the next day to tell me."

"Really," said Odette.

"You have to understand midwestern Jews: They're afraid of being found out. They're afraid of being discovered." He breathed steadily, in and out, and the window shade flapped a little from being over the radiator. "As you probably know already, my parents were killed in the camps."

Odette did not say anything, and then she said, "Yes. I know." And at the moment she said it, she realized she did know, somehow had known it all along, though the fact of it had stayed beneath the surface, gilled and swimming like a fish, and now had burst up, gasping, with its mouth wide.

"Are you really leaving on Friday?" he asked.

"What?"

"Friday. Are you?"

"I'm sorry, I just didn't hear what you said. There's wind outside or something."

"I asked you if you were really leaving on Friday."

"Oh," she said. She pressed her face hard into his neck. "Why don't you come with me?"

He laughed wearily. "Sure," he said. "All right," knowing better than she at that moment the strange winding line between charity and irony, between shoplifting and love.

During that last day she thought of nothing but him. She packed and cleaned out her little apartment, but she had done this so often now in her life, it didn't mean anything, not in the pit of her, not anything she might have wanted it to mean.

She should stay.

She should stay here with him, unorphan him with love's unorphaning, live wise and simple in a world monstrous enough for years of whores and death, and poems of whores and death, so monstrous how could one live in it at all? One had to build shelters. One had to make pockets and live inside them. She should live where there were trees. She should live where there were birds. No bird, no tree had ever made her unhappy.

But it would be like going to heaven and not finding any of your friends there. Her life would go all beatific and empty in the eyes. And if he came to New York, well, it would bewilder him. He had never been before, and no doubt he'd spend all his time staring up at the skyscrapers and exclaiming, "Gosh, look how tall those suckers are!" He would slosh through the vagrant urine, shoelaces untied. He would walk through the dog shit awaiting him like mines. He would read the menus in the windows of restaurants and whistle at the prices. He would stare at a sidewalk drunk, prone and spread-eagled and fumbling at the crotch, and he would say, not unkindly, "That guy's really got his act together." He would look at the women.

And her restlessness would ripple, double, a flavor of something cold. She would turn from him in bed, her hands under the pillow, the digital clock peeling back the old skins of numbers. She would sigh a little for the passage of time, the endless corridor of it, how its walls washed by you on either side—darkly, fast, and ever, ever.

"WHAT DO YOU DO, you stay overnight on the road somewhere?" he said, standing next to her car in the cold. It was Friday morning and spitting snow. He had come over and helped her load up the car.

"I drive until dark, then I check into a motel room and read until I fall asleep. Then I get up at six and drive some more."

"So, like, what are you bringing with you to read?" he asked. He seemed unhappy.

She had a *Vogue* magazine and *The Portable Jung*. "Something by Jung," she said.

"Jung?" he asked. His face went blank.

"Yeah," she sighed, not wanting to explain. "A book he wrote called *The Portable Jung*." She added, "He's a psychologist."

Pinky looked her deeply in the eyes. "I know," he said.

"You do?" She was a little surprised.

"Yeah. You should read his autobiography. It has a very interesting title."

She smiled. "Who *are* you? His autobiography? Really?"

"Yeah," said Pinky slowly. "It's called *Jung at Heart*."

She laughed loud, to please him. Then she looked at his face, to fix him like this in her mind. He was wearing a black shirt, a black sweater, black pants. He was smiling. "You look like Zorro today," she said, strangely moved. The spidery veins at his temples seemed like things under water, tentacular and drowned. She kissed him, long and at the rim of his ear, feeling in the rolls and spaces of her brain a winding, winding line. She got into the car. Though she hadn't even started up the engine, her departure had already happened, without her, ahead of her, so that what she now felt was the taunt of being left behind, of having to repeat, to imitate, of having to do it again, and now, and again.

"All this wandering that you do," he said, leaning in the window, his face white as a cream cheese, his scar the carved zigzag of a snowmobile across a winter lake. Wind blew handsomely through his hair. "How will anyone ever get close to you?"

"I don't know," she said. She shook his hand through the window and then put on her gloves.

And she thought about this all across Indiana, beneath the Easter hat of sunset that lit the motel roof in Sandusky, through the dawn of Pennsylvania, into which she soared like a birth—like someone practicing to be born. There were things she'd forget: a nightgown stuck on a hook behind the bathroom door, earrings on the motel nightstand. And all love that had overtaken her would have to be a memory, a truck on the interstate roaring up from the left, a thing she must let pass.

She would park the car right off Delancey Street; there would be a spot across the street from the hotel with the Pepsi sign and HOTEL in lights beneath. All night, sirens would keen, and traffic would whoosh and grind its way down Houston, down Canal, toward the Holland Tunnel—a bent sign to which aimed straight at her window. She would get up in the morning and go for sundries; at the corner bodega the clerk would mis-press the numbers on the register, and the toothpaste would ring up at $2,000. "Two thousand dollars!" the clerk would howl, standing back and looking at Odette. "Get a *real* tooth-paste!" From a long distance, and at night, a man would phone to say, doubtfully, "I should come visit on Valentine's," history of all kinds, incongruous and mangling itself, eating its own lips.

If she had spurned gifts from fate or God or some earnest substitute, she would never feel it in that way. She felt like someone of whom she was fond, an old and future friend of herself, still unspent and up ahead somewhere, like a light that moves.

# Starving
# Again

DENNIS'S EX-WIFE had fallen in love with a man she said was like out of a book. Dennis forgot to ask what book. He was depressed and barely dating. "I should have said to her, 'Yeah, and what book?' " Dennis was always kicking himself on the phone, not an easy thing, the tricky ouch of it. His friend Mave tended to doodle a lot when talking to him, slinky items with features, or a solitary game of tick-tack-toe. Sometimes she even interrupted him to ask what time it was. Her clock was in the other room.

"But you know," Dennis was saying, "I've got my own means of revenge: If she wants to go out with other men, I'm going to sit here and just let her."

"That's an incredibly powerful form of revenge," said Mave. She was not good on the phone. She needed the face, the pattern of eyes, nose, trembling mouth. When she was on the phone she often had to improvise Dennis's face from a window: the pug nose of the lock, the paned eyes, the lip jut of the sill. Or else she drew another slinky item with features. People talking were meant to look at a face, the disastrous cupcake of it, the hide-and-seek of the heart dashing across. With a phone, you said words, but you never watched them go in. You saw them off at the airport but never knew whether there was anyone there to greet them when they got off the plane.

They met for dinner at some sort of macrobiotic place, because Dennis had recently become obsessed. Before his wife left him, his idea of eating healthy had been to go to McDonald's and order the Filet-o-Fish, but now he had whole books about miso. And about tempeh. Mostly, however, he had books about love. He believed in studying his own heart this way. Men were like that, Mave had noticed. They liked to look in the mirror. For women, mirrors were a chore: Women looked, frowned, got out equipment, and went to work. But for men mirrors were sex: Men locked gazes with their own reflections, undressed themselves with their eyes, and stared for a shockingly long time. Mave believed that not being able to see your life clearly, to scrutinize it intelligently, meant that probably you were at the dead center of it, and that couldn't possibly be a bad thing.

This month Dennis was reading books written supposedly for women, titles like *Get Real, Smarting Cookie, Get Real* and *Why I Hate Myself*. "Those books are trouble," said Mave. "Too many well-adjusted people will endanger the arts in this country. To say nothing of the professions." She studied Dennis's flipped-over tie, the soft, torn eye of its clipped label. "You choose to be healthy, and you leave too many good people behind."

But Dennis said he identified, that the books were amazing, and he reached into the book bag he now carried with him everywhere and read passages aloud. "Here," he said to Mave, who had brought her own whiskey to the place and was pouring it into a water glass from which she had drunk all the water and left only the ice. She had had to argue with the waitress to get ice. "Oh, no—here," Dennis said. He had found another passage from *Why I Hate Myself* and started to read it, loud and with expression, when suddenly he broke into a disconsolate weep, deep and from the belly. "Oh, God, I'm sorry."

Mave shoved her whiskey glass across the table toward him. "Don't worry about it," she murmured. He took a sip, then put the book away. He dug through his book bag and found Kleenex to dab at his nose.

"I didn't get like this on my own," he said. "There are people responsible." Inside his bag Mave could see a newsmagazine with the exasperated headline: ETHIOPIA: WHY ARE THEY STARVING THIS TIME?

"Boredom is heartless," said Dennis, the tears slowing. He indicated the magazine. "When the face goes into a yawn, the blood to the chest gets constricted."

"Are you finished with my drink?"

"No." He took another gulp and winced. "I mean, yes," and he handed it back to Mave, wiped his mouth with a napkin. Mave looked at Dennis's face and was glad no one had broken up with her recently. When someone broke up with you, you became very unattractive, and it confirmed all the doubts that person had ever had about you to begin with. "Wait, just one more sip." Someone broke up with you and you yelled. You blistered, withered, and flushed. You apologized to inanimate objects and drank when you swore you wouldn't. You went around humming the theme to *Valley of the Dolls*, doing all the instruments even, lingering on the line about *gotta get off, gonna get, have to get. . . .* It wasn't good to go out on that kind of limb for love. You went out on a limb for food, but not for love. Love was not food. Love, thought Mave, was more like the rest rooms at the Ziegfeld: sinks in the stalls, big deal. Mave worked hard to forget very quickly afterward what the men she went out with even looked like. This was called sticking close to the trunk.

"All yours," said Dennis. He was smiling now. The whiskey brought the blood to his face in a nice way.

Mave looked down at her menu. "There's no spaghetti and meatballs here. I wanted to order the child's portion of the spaghetti and meatballs."

"Oh, that reminds me," said Dennis, shaking a finger for emphasis. With his books away and the whiskey in him, he seemed more confident. "Did I tell you the guy my wife's seeing is Italian? Milanese, not Brooklyn. What do you suppose that means, her falling in love with an Italian?"

"It means she's going to feel scruffy all the time. It means that he will stare at all the fuzzies on her shirt while she is telling him something painful about a childhood birthday party nobody came to. Let's face it: She's going to start to miss the fact, Dennis, that your hair zooms out all over the goddamn place."

"I'm getting it cut tomorrow."

Mave put on her reading glasses. "This is not a restaurant. Restaurants serve different things from this."

"You know, one thing about these books for women, I have to tell you. The whole emphasis on locating and accepting your homosexual side is really very powerful. It frees and expands some other sort of love in you."

Mave looked up at him and smiled. She was drawn to the insane because of their blazing minds. "So you've located and accepted?"

"Well, I've realized this. I like boys. *And* I like girls." He leaned toward her confidentially. "I just don't like *berls*." Dennis reached again for Mave's whiskey. "Of course, I am completely in the wrong town. May I?" He leaned his head back, and the ice cubes knocked against his teeth. Water beaded up on his chin. "So, Mave, who are *you* romancing these days?" Dennis was beginning to look drunk. His lips were smooth and thick and hung open like a change purse.

"These days?" There were little ways like this of stalling for time.

"These right here."

"Right here. These. I've been seeing Mitch again a little."

Dennis dropped his forehead into his palm, which had somehow flown up from the table, so that the two met midair in an unsightly smack. "Mitch! Mave, he's such a womanizer!"

"So I needed to be womanized. I was losing my sheen."

"You know what you do? You get all your boyfriends on sale. It's called Bargain Debasement. Immolation by desire."

"Look, you need to be womanized, you go to a womanizer. I don't take these things seriously anymore. I make it a point now to forget what everybody looks like. I'm being Rudolf Bing. I've lost my mind and am traipsing around the South Seas with an inappropriate lover, and I believe in it. I think everybody in a love affair is being Rudolf Bing anyway, and they're vain to believe otherwise. . . . Oh, my God, that man in the sweater is feeling his girlfriend's lymph nodes." Mave put away her reading glasses and fumbled around in her bag for the whiskey flask. That was the thing with hunger: It opened up something dangerous in you, something endless, like a universe, or a cliff. "I'm sorry. Rudolf Bing is on my mind. He's really been on my mind. I feel like we're all almost like him."

"Almost like Bing in love," said Dennis. *"What a day this has been. What a rare mood I'm in."* Mave was in a long sip. "I've been listening to that *Live at Carnegie Hall* tape too much."

"Music! Let's talk about music! Or death! Why do we always have to talk about love?"

"Because our parents were sickos, and we're starved for it."

"You know what I've decided? I don't want to be cremated. I used to, but now I think it sounds just a little too much like a blender speed. Now I've decided I want to be embalmed, and then I want a plastic surgeon to come put in silicone implants everywhere. Then I want to be laid out in the woods like Snow White, with a gravestone that reads *Gotta Dance*." The whiskey was going down sweet. That was what happened after a while, with no meal to assist—it had to do the food work on its own. "There. We talked about death."

"That's talking about death?"

"What is *kale?* I don't understand why they haven't taken our order yet. I mean, it's crowded now, but it wasn't ten minutes ago. Maybe it was the ice thing."

"You know what else my wife says about this Italian? She says he goes around singing this same song to himself. You know what it is?"

" 'Santa Lucia.' "

"No. It's the 'Addams Family' theme song: *Their house is a museum, when people come to see-um . . .*"

"Your wife tells you this?"

"We're friends."

"Don't tell me you're friends. You hate her."

"We're friends. I don't hate her."

"You think she's a user and a tart. She's with some guy with great shoes whose coif doesn't collapse into hairpin turns across his part."

"You used to be a nice person."

"I never was a nice person. I'm still a nice person."

"I don't like this year," said Dennis, his eyes welling again.

"I know," said Mave. "Eighty-eight. It's too Sergio Mendes or something."

"You know, it's OK not to be a nice person."

"I need your permission? Thank you." This was what Dennis had been doing lately: granting everyone permission to feel the way they were going to feel regardless. It was the books. Dennis's relationship to his own feelings had become tender, curatorial. Dismantling. Entomological. Mave couldn't be like that. She treated her emotional life the way she treated her car: She let it go, let it tough it out. To friends she said things like "I know you're thinking this looks like a '79, but it's really an '87." She finally didn't care to understand all that much about her emotional life; she just went ahead and did it. The point, she thought, was to attend the meager theater of it, quietly, and not stand up in the middle and shout, "Oh, my God, you can see the crew backstage!" There was a point at which the study of something became a frightening and naive thing.

"But, Dennis, really, why do you think so much about love, of someone loving you or not loving you? That is all you read about, all you talk about."

"Put the starving people of the world together in a room, and what you get is a lot of conversation about roast beef. They should be talking about the Napoleonic Code?" At the mention of roast beef, Mave's face lit up, greenish, fluorescent. She looked past Dennis and saw the waitress coming toward their table at last, she was moving slowly, meanly, scowling. There was a large paper doily stuck to her shoe. "I mean . . ." Dennis was saying, looking pointedly at Mave, but Mave was watching the waitress approach. *Oh, life, oh, sweet, forgiven for the ice . . .* He grabbed Mave's wrist. There was always an emergency. And then there was love. And then there was another emergency. That was the sandwiching of it. Emergency. Love. Emergency. "I mean, it's not as if you've been dozing off," Dennis was saying, his voice reaching her now, high and watery. "I mean, correct me if I'm wrong," he said, "but I don't think I've been having this conversation alone." He tightened his grip. "I mean, have I?"

# Like
# Life

*Everybody likes the circus.*
*Clowns! elephants! trained horses! peanuts!*
*Everybody likes the circus.*
*Acrobats! tight-rope walkers! camels! band music!*
*Suppose you had a choice of going to the circus*
*or painting a picture. Which would you choose?*
*You'd choose the circus.*
*Everybody likes the circus.*
      —V. M. Hillyer and E. G. Huey,
         *A Child's History of Art*

ALL THE MOVIES that year were about people
with plates in their heads: Spirits from another galaxy gather
in a resort town at night, taking over the townspeople—all but
the man with the plate in his head. Or: A girl with a plate in
her head wanders a city beach, believing she is someone else.
Evidence washes up on shore. There are sailors. Or: A woman
dreams of a beautiful house in which no one lives, and one day
she passes the actual house—a cupola, gables, and a porch. She
walks up to it, knocks on the door, and it is opened slowly by

her! a woman who is a twin of herself, grinning. She has a plate in her head.

Life seemed to have become like that. It had burst out of itself, like a bug.

In February a thaw gave the city the weepy ooze of a wound. There were many colds, people coughing in the subways. The sidewalks foamed to a cheese of spit, and the stoops, doorways, bus shelters were hedged with Rosies—that is what they were called—the jobless men, women, children with gourd lumps or fevers, imploring, hating eyes, and puffed lavender mouths, stark as paintings of mouths. The Rosies sold flowers: a prim tulip, an overflowing iris. Mostly no one bought any. Mostly it was just other Rosies, trading bloom for bloom, until one of them, a woman or a child, died in the street, the others gathering around in a wail, in the tiny, dark morning hours, which weren't morning at all but night.

THAT YEAR was the first that it became illegal—for those who lived in apartments or houses—not to have a television. The government claimed that important information, information necessary for survival, might need to be broadcast automatically, might need simply to burst on, which it could do. Civilization was at stake, it was said. "Already at the stake," said others, who had come to suspect that they were being spied on, controlled, that what they had thought when they were little— that the people on the television could also see you—now was true. You were supposed to leave it plugged in at all times, the plastic antenna raised in a V—for victory or peace, no one could say.

Mamie lost sleep. She began to distrust things, even her own words; too much had moved in. Objects implanted in your body—fillings, earrings, contraceptives—like satellite dishes, could be picking up messages, substituting their words for yours, feeding you lines. You never knew. Open your mouth, it might betray you with lies, with lackadaise, with moods and speak not your own. The things you were saying might be old radio programs bounced off the foil of your molars, or taxi calls fielded by the mussely glove of your ear. What you described as real might be only a picture, something from *Life* magazine you were forced to live out, after the photography, in imitation. Whole bodies, perhaps, could be ventriloquized. Approximated. You could sit on the lap of a thing and just move your lips. You could become afraid. You could become afraid someone was making you afraid: a new fear, like a gourmet's, a paranoid's paranoia.

This was not the future. This was what was with you now in the house.

Mamie lived in a converted beauty parlor storefront—a tin ceiling, a stench of turpentine, and extra sinks. At night her husband, a struggling painter, moody and beer-breathed, lay sleeping next to her, curled against her, an indifferent whistle in his nose. She closed her eyes. *What all to love in the world*, went a prayer from her childhood. What all to love?

The lumber of his bones piled close.

The radiator racked and spitting. Heat flapping like birds up the pipes.

SHE REMAINED AWAKE. On nights when she did sleep, her dreams were about the end of life. They involved getting somewhere, getting to the place where she was supposed to die, where it was OK. She was always in a group, like a fire drill or a class trip. Can we die here? Are we there yet? Which way can it possibly be?

Or else there was the house dream. Always the house dream, like the movie of the dream of the house. She would find a house, knock on the door, and it would open slowly, a wedge of dark, and then stop, her own profile greeting her, hanging there midair like a chandelier.

*Death*, said her husband, Rudy. He kept a small hatchet under the mattress, in case of intruders. *Death*. Last year she had gone to a doctor, who had looked at her throat and a mole on her back, studying them like Rorschachs for whatever he might see in them. He removed the mole and put it floating in a pathologist's vial, a tiny marine animal. Peering in at her throat, he said, "Precancer"—like a secret or a zodiac sign.

"*Pre*cancer?" she had repeated quietly, for she was a quiet woman. "Isn't that . . . like *life?*" She was sitting, and he was standing. He fumbled with some alcohol and cotton balls, which he kept on the counter in kitcheny-looking jars, the flour and sugar of the medical world.

He took her wrist and briefly squeezed. "It's *like* life, but it's not *necessarily* life."

THERE WAS a wrought-iron fence all around and a locked gate, but it was the bird feeder she remarked first, the wooden arms, the open mouth of boards stuck up there on a single leg. It was nearing Valentine's Day, an angry slosh of a morning, and she was on her way to a realtor, a different one this time, not far from the Fourth and Smith stop of the F train—from where you could see the Statue of Liberty. On her way, she had come upon a house with a bird feeder. A bird feeder! And a tree in front, a towering oak, over one hundred fifty years old. A grade school teacher had brought her class to it and now stood in front of it, pointing and saying, "A hundred and fifty years ago. Can anyone tell me when that was?"

But it was the bird feeder, initially: a cross with an angle-roofed shelter at the head—a naked scarecrow bedecked with horizontals like a Frank Lloyd Wright house, or an alpine motel, its wooden ledges strewn with millet seed. In the freckled snow below lay tiny condiment cups of peanut butter, knocked to the ground. A flibberty squirrel, hopping and pausing in spasms, lifted each cup to his nose and nibbled. On the feeder itself was a pair of pigeons—lidless, thick-necked, municipal gargoyles; but there, wasn't that also a sparrow? And a grosbeak?

The house was a real house, one of the few left in New York. A falling-down Edwardian Gothic with a cupola, once painted a silvery gray and now chipping. There was a porch and latticework of carpenter's lace—a house one would go to for piano lessons, if people still took piano lessons, a house invariably seized for a funeral home. It was squeezed between two storefronts—the realtor's and a laundromat.

"You're looking for a one-bedroom?" said the realtor.

"Yes," said Mamie, though it suddenly seemed both too little and too much to ask for. The realtor had the confident hair and makeup of a woman who had lived forever in New York, a woman who knew ever so wearily how to tie a scarf. Mamie studied the realtor's scarf, guessing the exact geometry of the folds, the location of the knot. If Mamie ever had surgery, scars in a crisscross up her throat, she would have to know such things. A hat, a scarf, a dot of rouge, mints in the mouth: Everyone in New York was hiding something, eventually.

The real estate agent took out an application form. She picked up a pen. "Your name?"

"Mamie Cournand."

"*What?* Here. You fill this out."

It was pretty much the same form she'd filled out previously at other agencies. What sort of apartment are you looking for; how much do you make; how do you make it . . . ?

"What is children's historical illustrator?" deadpanned the realtor. "If you don't mind me asking."

"I, uh, work on a series of history publications, picture books actually, for chil—"

"Free lance?" She looked at Mamie with doubt, suspicion, and then with sympathy to encourage candor.

"It's for the McWilliams Company." She began to lie. "I've got an office there that I use. The address is written here." She rose slightly from her seat, to point it out.

The realtor pulled away. "I'm oriented," she said.

"Oriented?"

"You don't need to reach and point. This your home and work phone? This your age . . . ? You forgot to put in your age."

"Thirty-five."

"Thirty-five," she repeated, writing it in. "You look younger." She looked at Mamie. "What are you willing to pay?"

"Um, up to nine hundred or so."

"Good luck," she snorted, and still seated in her caster-wheeled chair, she trundled over to the file cabinet, lifted out a manila folder, flipped it open. She placed Mamie's application on top. "This isn't the eighties anymore, you know."

Mamie cleared her throat. Deep in the back she could feel the wound sticking there, unhealed. "It hasn't not been for very long. I mean, just a few years." The awkward, frightened look had leaped to her eyes again, she knew. Fear making a child of her face—she hated this in herself. As a girl, she had always listened in a slightly stricken way and never spoke unless she was asked a question. When she was in college she was the kind of student sometimes too anxious to enter the cafeteria. Often she just stayed in her room and drank warm iced tea from a mix and a Hot Pot. "You live right over here?" The realtor motioned behind her. "Why are you moving?"

"I'm leaving my husband."

The corner of her mouth curled. "*In this day and age?* Good luck." She shrugged and spun around to dig through files again. There was a long silence, the realtor shaking her head.

Mamie craned her neck. "I'd like to see what you have, at any rate."

"We've got nothing." The realtor slammed the file drawer

and twisted back around. "But keep trying us. We might have something tomorrow. We're expecting some listings then."

THEY HAD BEEN married for fourteen years, living on Brooklyn's south slope for almost ten. It was a neighborhood once so Irish that even as late as the fifties, kids had played soccer in the street and shouted in Gaelic. When she and Rudy first moved in, the area was full of Italian men who barely knew Italian and leaned out of the windows of private clubs, shouting "How aw ya?" Now Hispanic girls in bright leotards gathered on the corner after school, smoking cigarettes and *scoming* the streets. *Scoming*, said the boys. Artists had taken up residence, as well as struggling actors, junkies, desperate Rosies in the street. *Watch out*, went the joke, *for the struggling actors*.

Mamie and Rudy's former beauty parlor now had a padlocked door and boarded front windows. Inside remained the original lavender walls, the gold metallic trim. They had built a loft at one end of the place, and at the other were bookcases, easels, canvases, and a drawing table. Stacked against the wall by the door were Rudy's huge paintings of snarling dogs and Virgin Marys. He had a series of each, and hoped, before he died, *before I shoot myself in the head on my fortieth birthday*, to have a gallery. Until then he painted apartments or borrowed money from Mamie. He was responsible for only one bill—utilities—and on several occasions had had to rush out to intercept Con Ed men arriving with helmets and boots to disconnect the electricity. "Never a dull moment," Rudy would say, thrusting cash into their hands. Once he had tried to pay the bill with two small still lifes.

"You don't think about the real world, Rudy. There's a real world out there." There was in him, she felt, only a fine line between insanity and charm. "A real world about to explode."

"You don't think I worry about the world *exploding*?" His expression darkened. "You don't think I get tears in my eyes every fucking day thinking about those Rembrandts at the Met and what's going to happen to them when it does?"

"Rudy, I went to a realtor today."

Probably in their marriage she had been too dreamy and inconsistent. For love to last, you had to have illusions or have no illusions at all. But you had to stick to one or the other. It was the switching back and forth that endangered things.

"Again?" Rudy sighed, ironic but hurt. Once love had seemed like magic. Now it seemed like tricks. You had to learn the sleight-of-hand, the snarling dog, the Hail Marys and hoops of it! Through all the muck of themselves, the times they had unobligated each other, the anger, the permitted absences, the loneliness grown dangerous, she had always returned to him. He'd had faith in that—abracadabra! But eventually the dead-liness set in again. Could you live in the dead excellence of a thing—the stupid mortar of a body, the stubborn husk love had crawled from? Yes, he thought.

The television flashed on automatically, one of the govern-ment ads: pretty couples testifying to their undying devotion, undying bodies. "We are the Undying," they said, and they cuddled their children, who had freckles that bled together on the cheeks, and toys with glassy button eyes. *Undying*, the commercials said. *Be undying.* "I can't bear it," Mamie said. "I can't bear the brother and sister of us. I can't bear the mother and son of us. I can't bear the Undying commercials. I can't bear washing my hair in dishwashing liquid, or doing the dishes in cheap shampoo, because we're too broke or disorganized or depressed to have both at the same time." Always, they'd made do. For toilet paper they used holiday-imprinted napkins—cocktail napkins with poinsettias on them. A big box of them, with a tray, had been sent to Rudy by mistake. For towels they used bath mats. For bath mats more poinsettia napkins. They bought discount soaps with sayings on the label like *Be gentle and you need not be strong.* "We're camping out here, Rudy. This is camping!" She tried to appeal to something he would understand. "My work. It's affecting my work. Look at this!" and she went over to a small drawing table and held up her half-finished sketch of Squanto planting corn. She'd been attempting a nuclear metaphor: white man learning to plant things in the ground, which would later burst forth; how the white man had gotten carried away with planting. "He looks like a toad."

"He looks like a catcher for the Boston Red Sox." Rudy smiled. Would she smile? He grew mock-serious: "The faculties of discernment and generosity are always at war. You must decide whether you will be muse or artist. A woman cannot be both."

"I can't believe you," she said, staring accusingly around their apartment. "This is not life. This is something else," and the whole ill-lit place stared back at her, hurt, a ditzy old beauty parlor flunking someone else's math.

"Forget this Squanto thing," he said, looking compassionate. "I've got an idea for you. I've thought about it all day: a children's book called *Too Many Lesbians.*" He began motioning with his arms. "Lesbians in bushes, lesbians in trees . . . *Find the lesbians . . .*"

"I'm going out for some air," she said, and she grabbed her coat and flew out the door. It was evening already, zinc gray and chill, the puddles freezing on the walks in a thin glaze. She hurried past the shivering Rosies at the corner, hurried six blocks in a zigzag to look at the bird feeder again. Visit a place at night, she knew, and it was yours.

When she reached it, the house was dark, holding its breath, soundless so as not to be discovered. She pressed her face against the gate, the hard cilia of its ironwork, and sighed, longing for another existence, one that belonged to a woman who lived in a house like this, the lovely brow of its mansard roof, thoughtful with rooms. She felt a distrust of her own life, like those aerospace engineers reluctant to fly in planes of their own design, fearing death by their own claptrappery.

The bird feeder stood tall as a constable. There were no birds.

"YOU SHOULD never leave. You just always come back," whispered Rudy. *A tourist in your own despair,* he had once said. It was the title of one of his paintings. One of a snarling dog leaping over a sofa.

She stared through the small window by their bed, a strip of sky and one dim star, an asterisk to take her away briefly to an explanation—the night bragging a footnote. He held her, kissed her. Here in bed was when he seemed to her not to be doing imitations of other people. After fifteen years, she had seen all the imitations—friends, parents, movie actors—until it was a little scary, as if he were many different people at once, people to turn to, not in distress, but like a channel on television, a mind gone crazy with cable. He was Jimmy Stewart. He was Elvis Presley. "When you were growing up, were your parents funny?" she asked him once.

"*My parents?* You've got to be kidding," he said. "I mean, once in a while they *memorized* something." He was Dylan on the harmonica. Lifelike; absolutely lifelike. He was James Cagney. He was some musical blend he called Smokey Robinson Caruso.

"Don't you think we'd have beautiful children?" Rudy now pleaded, sleepily, his hand smoothing the bangs off her brow.

"They'd be nervous and insane," she murmured.

"You're strung out about your health."

"But maybe they'd also be able to do imitations."

Rudy kissed her throat, her ears, her throat again. She had to spit daily into a jar she kept in the bathroom, and to visit the clinic regularly, bringing the jar.

"You think we don't love each other anymore," he said. He was capable of tenderness. Though sometimes he was rough, pressing himself upon her with a force that startled her, wanting to make love and kissing her meanly against the wall: *come on, come on*; though his paintings had grown more violent, feverish swirls of men in business suits sodomizing animals: *this is my statement about yuppies, OK?*; though in coffee shops he often lorded over her spells of sorrowful boredom by looking disgusted while she blinked soggily into her lunch—here without his clothes on, with her face open to him, he could be a tender husband. "You think that, but it's not true." Years ago she had come to know his little lies, harmless for the most part and born of vanity and doubts, and sometimes fueled merely by a desire to hide from things whose truth took too much effort to figure out. She knew the way he would tell the same anecdotes from his life, over and over again, each time a little differently, the exaggerations and contradictions sometimes having a par- ticular purpose—his self-portrait as Undiscovered Genius—and sometimes not seeming to have one at all. "Six inches from the door was an empty shopping cart jammed up against the door," he told her once, and she said, "Rudy, how can it be six inches from the door but also jammed up against it?"

"It was full of newspapers and tin cans, stuff like that. I don't know."

She couldn't even say when the love between them had begun to sicken, how long it had been gasping drearily over its own grave of rage and obligation. They had spent over a third of their lives together—a third, like sleep. He was the only man who had ever, even once, claimed to find her beautiful. And he had stuck with her, loved her, even when she was twenty and in terrified thrall to sex, not daring to move, out of po- liteness or was it timidity. He had helped her. Later she learned to crave the drugged heart of sex, the drugs at the core of it: All the necessary kissing and fussing seemed only that—necessary—to get to the drugs. But it had all been with Rudy, always with him. "Now we are truly in cahoots," she exulted, the day they were married at the county clerk's.

"I don't look good in cahoots," he said, his arm swung loosely around. "Let's go get tattoos."

What kisses there were in disappointment; sorrow fueled them, pushed them to a place. The city writhed, and the world shut down all around. Rudy gave pouting mouths to his Virgin Marys, popped open cans of beer, watched old movies on TV. *"You are happy until you say you are happy. Then you are no longer happy.* Bonnard. The great painter of happiness articulating itself to death."

Maybe she'd thought life would provide her with something more lasting, more flattering than sexual love, but it never had, not really. For a while, she'd felt like one of the girls on the street corner: a world of leotards and drugs—drugs you hungered for and got to fast.

"Don't you think we have a very special love?" asked Rudy. But she wasn't believing in special love. Even when everyone was being practical, she believed—like a yearning for wind in winter—in only one kind of love, the kind in art: where you die for it. She had read too many books, said Rudy, Victorian novels where the children spoke in the subjunctive. *You take too much to heart,* he wrote her once, when she was away, living in Boston with an aging aunt and a sketch pad.

"I would never die for you," she said softly.

"Sure you would," said Rudy. He sighed, lay back. "Do you want a glass of water? I'll get down and get it."

At times her marriage seemed like a saint, guillotined and still walking for miles through the city, carrying its head. She often thought of the whole apartment going up in flames. What would she take with her? What few things would she grab for her new life? The thought exhilarated her. *You take too much to heart.*

. . .

IN THE HOUSE DREAM, she walks in past the gate and the bird feeder and knocks on the door. It opens slowly and she steps in, in and around, until it is she herself who is opening it, from the other side, wondering who has knocked.

"*Death*," said Rudy again. "Death by nuclear holocaust. Everyone's having those dreams. Except for me. I'm having these completely embarrassing nightmares about bad haircuts and not knowing anyone at a party."

In the morning, sun spilled in through the window by the bed. There was more light in the apartment in winter when there was snow on their overhang and it reflected sunlight inward, making garnet of the rug and striping the bed. A stray tomcat they had befriended, taken in, and fed lounged on the sill. They called him Food Man or Bill of the Baskervilles, and occasionally Rudy was kind to him, lifting the cat up high so that it could check out the bookcases, sniff the ceiling, which it liked to do. Mamie put birdseed out in the snow to attract pigeons, who would amuse the cat through the glass when he was inside. Cat TV. Rudy, she knew, hated pigeons, their lizard feet and pea brains, their strangely bovine meanness. He admired his friend Marco, who had put metal stakes outside on his air conditioner to keep pigeons from landing there.

Ordinarily Mamie was the first one up, the one to make coffee, the one to head cautiously down the makeshift rungs hammered in the side post, the one to pad out to the kitchen area, heat up water, rinse out mugs, brew coffee, get juice, and bring it all back to bed. This was how they had breakfast, the bedclothes a calico of spills.

But today, as on the other days he feared she would leave him, Rudy wormed naked out of the covers before her, jackknifed at the loft's edge, descended to the floor with a thump. Mamie watched his body: lanky, big-eared; his back, his arms, his hips. No one ever talked about a man's hips, the hard twin saddles of them. He put on a pair of boxer shorts. "I like these underwear," he said. "They make me feel like David Niven."

He made coffee from water they stored in a plastic garbage barrel. They had it delivered this way, weekly, like seltzer, and they paid twenty dollars for it. They washed dishes in the water that came through the faucets, and they even took quick showers in it, though they risked rashes, said the government doctors. Once Mamie hadn't heard a special radio warning and had taken a shower, scrubbing hard with an old biscuit of loofah, only to step out with burning welts on her arms and shoulders: There had been a chemical pumped into the water, she learned later, one thought to impede the growth of viruses from river-rat fleas. She had soothed her skin with mayonnaise, which was all they had, and the blisters peeled open to a pink ham flesh beneath.

Except for the pleasure of Rudy bringing her coffee—the gift of it—she hated this place. But you could live with a hate. She had. It was so powerful, it had manners; it moved to one side most of the time to let you pass. It was mere dislike that clouded and nagged and stepped in front of your spirit, like a child wanting something.

Rudy returned with the coffee. Mamie rolled to the bed's edge and took the poinsettia tray from him, as he climbed back up and over her. "It's the Coffee Man," she said, trying to sound cheerful, perhaps even to chirp. Shouldn't she try? She placed the tray between them, picked up her coffee, and sipped. It was funny: With each swallow she could recast this fetid place, resee it with a caffeinated heart's eye, make it beautiful even. But it would be the drizzle of affection felt for a hated place before you left it. And she would leave. Again. She would turn the walls and sinks and the turpentined dust to a memory, make it the scene of mild crimes, and think of it with a false, willowy love.

But then you could get to calling everything false and willowy and never know anymore what was true and from the heart.

The cat came and curled up next to her. She massaged the cool, leathery wafer of its ear and plucked dust from its whiskers. He cocked his head and closed his eyes sleepily, content. How sad, she thought, how awful, how fortunate to be an animal and mistake grooming for love.

She placed a hand on Rudy's arm. He bent his head to kiss it, but then couldn't bend that far without spilling his coffee, and so straightened up again.

"Are you ever lonely?" Mamie asked him. Every moment of a morning seemed battled for, the past and future both seeking custody. She laid her cheek against his arm.

"Mamie," he said softly, and that was all.

In the last five years almost all of their friends had died.

*The Indians weren't used to the illnesses that the English brought with them to the new world. Many Indians got sick. When they got chicken pox or mumps, they sometimes died. A very proud Indian might happen to wake up one morning and look in the mirror he'd gotten from an English trader and see red spots polka-dotting his face! The proud Indian would be very upset. He might hurl himself against a tree to maim himself. Or he might throw himself over a cliff or into a fire* (picture).

THE AGENT had on a different scarf today—a turquoise jacquard, twisted into a long coil that she wore wrapped around her neck like a collar. "A room," she said quickly. "Would you settle for a room?"

"I'm not sure," said Mamie. When she spoke with someone snappy and high-powered like that, she felt depressed and under siege.

"Well, come back when you are," said the agent, in her chair, trundling toward the files.

Mamie took the train into Manhattan. She would walk around the art galleries in SoHo, after she dropped off a manuscript at the McWilliams Company. Then she would come back home via the clinic. She had her glass jar in her purse.

In the McWilliams bathroom was a secretary named Goz, whom Mamie had spoken to a few times. Goz was standing in front of the mirror, applying eye makeup. "Hey, how ya doin'?" she said, when she saw Mamie.

Mamie stood next to her, washed her face off from the subway, and dug through her purse for a hairbrush. "I'm OK. How are you?"

"All right." Goz sighed. She had two wax perfume wands, mascara, and several colors of eye shadow spread out on the mirror ledge. She scrutinized her own reflection and sucked in her cheeks. "You know, it's taken me years to get my eye makeup to look like this."

Mamie smiled sympathetically. "A lot of practice, huh."

"No—years of *eye makeup*. I let it build up."

Mamie leaned over and brushed her hair upside down.

"Hmmm," said Goz a little irritably. "What have you been doing these days?"

"Oh, a children's thing again. It's the first time I've done the pictures *and* the text." Mamie straightened and threw her head back. "I'm, um, dropping off a chapter for Seth today." Her hair fell around her face in a penumbra. She looked insane.

"Oh. Hmmm," said Goz. She was watching Mamie's hair with interest. "I like *neat* hair. I don't think a woman should look as if sex has already happened."

Mamie smiled at her. "How about you? You going out a lot, having fun?"

"Yeah," said Goz a little defensively. Everyone these days was defensive about their lives. Everyone had settled. "I'm going out. I'm going out with this *man*. And my friends are going out with these *men*. And sometimes we all go out together. The trouble is we're all about thirty years younger than these guys. We'll go to a restaurant or something and I'll look around the table and like every man at our table is thirty years older than his date."

"A father-daughter banquet," said Mamie, trying to joke. "We used to have those at our church."

Goz stared at her. "Yeah," she said, finally turning to put away all her makeup. "You still with that guy who lives in a beauty parlor?"

"Rudy. My husband."

"Whatever," said Goz, and she went into a stall and closed the door.

*None of the English seemed to be getting sick. This caused much whispering in the Indian villages. "We are dying," they said. "But they are not. How come?"*

*And so the chief, weak and ailing, would put on English clothes and go to the Englishmen* (picture).

"THIS IS for Seth Billets," Mamie said, handing the receptionist a large manila envelope. "If he has any questions, he can just phone me. Thanks." She turned and fled the building, taking the stairs rather than the elevator. She never liked to meet with Seth. He tended to be harried and abstracted, and they worked just as well together on the phone. "Mamie? Great stuff," he liked to say. "I'm sending the manuscript back with my suggestions. But ignore them." And always the manuscript arrived three weeks later with comments in the margin like *Oh please* and *No shit*.

She bought a paper and walked downtown toward some galleries she knew on Grand Street, stopping at a coffee shop on Lafayette. Usually she ordered a cup of coffee *and* a cup of tea, as well as a brownie, propping up her sadness with chocolate and caffeine so that it became an anxiety.

"You want something or nothing?" the waitress asked her.

"What?" Startled, Mamie ordered the Slenderella.

"Good choice," said the waitress, as if it had been a test, and then hurried to the kitchen in a palsied jog.

Mamie spread the paper out at a diagonal and read, the pages stoically full of news of the war in India and, locally, of the women's bodies dredged up weekly from the Gowanus Canal. Disappeared women, with contusions. Beaten and drowned. Secretaries, students, a Rosie or two.

The Slenderella came with egg salad, and she ate it slowly, dissolving it in her mouth, its moist, mothering yellow. On the obituary page there were different deaths, young men, as in a war, and always the ending: *He is survived by his parents*.

Leaving the paper on the table as a tip, she spent the rest of the morning wandering in and out of galleries, looking at paintings that seemed much worse to her than Rudy's. Why these and not her husband's? Painting pictures was the only thing he had ever wanted to do, but no one was helping him. Age had already grabbed him in the face: His cheeks sagged houndishly, his beard was shot with white. Bristly hairs sprouted like wheat from his ears. She used to go with him to art openings, listening to people say bewildering things like "Syntax? Don't you just love *syntax*?" or "Now you know why people are starving in India—we had to wait an hour for our biriyani!" She began to leave early—while he lingered there, dressed in a secondhand pair of black leather pants he looked terrible in, chatting up the dealers, the famous, the successful. He would offer to show them his slides. Or he would go into his rap about Theoretical Disaster Art, how if you can depict atrocities, you can prevent them. "Anticipate, and imitate," he said. "You can preclude and dispirit a holocaust by depriving it of its originality; enough books and plays and paintings, you can change history by getting there first."

One East Village dealer looked him heavily in the eye and

said, "You know, in a hive, when a bee has something to communicate, it does a dance. But if the bee does not stop dancing, the others sting it to death," and the dealer then turned and started talking to someone else.

Rudy always walked home alone, slow across the bridge, his life exactly the same as it was. His heart, she knew, was full of that ghetto desire to leap from poor to rich with a single, simple act, that yearning that exhausted the poor—something the city required: an exhausted poor. He would comb the dumpsters for clothes, for artbooks, for pieces of wood to build into frames and stretchers, and in the early hours of the morning he would arrive home with some huge dried flower he had scavenged, a wobbly plant stand, or a small, beveled mirror. At noon, without an apartment to paint, he might go into the city, to the corner of Broadway and Wall, to play his harmonica for coins. Sea chanteys and Dylan. Sometimes passersby would slow down on "Shenandoah," which he played so mournfully that even what he called "some plagiarist of living," in a beige all-weather coat, "some guy who wears his asshole on his sleeve," might stop on his lunch hour to let a part of himself leap up in the hearing, in communion, in reminder of times left behind. But mostly, everyone just sailed past, tense with errands, stubbing their feet on the shoe box Rudy'd placed on the sidewalk for contributions. He did not play badly. And he could look as handsome as an actor. But mad—something there in the eyes. Madmen, in fact, were attracted to him, came bounding up to him like buddies, shouting psychotically, shaking his hand and putting their arms around him while he played.

But people with money wouldn't give it to a guy with a harmonica. A guy with a harmonica had to be a drinker. To say nothing of a guy with a harmonica wearing a T-shirt that read: *Wino Cogito: I Think Therefore I Drink*. "I forget sometimes," said Rudy, unconvincingly. "I forget and wear that

88888888888888888888888888
8888888888888888

shirt." People with money would spend six dollars on a cocktail for themselves, but not eighty cents toward a draft beer for a guy with a shirt like that. Rudy would return home with enough cash for one new brush, and with that new brush would paint a picture of a bunch of businessmen sodomizing farm animals. "The best thing about figure painting," he liked to say, "is deciding what everyone will wear."

On days when he and his friend Marco got apartment-painting work, they would make real money, tax free, and treat themselves to Chinese food. They called their housepainting partnership We Aim for the Wall, and as a gimmick they gave out balloons. On these occasions rich people liked them—"Hey, where's my balloon, guys?"—until they discovered liquor missing or unfamiliar long-distance calls on their phone bills. As a result, referrals were rare.

And now something was happening to him. At night, even more than before, he would push her, force her, and she was growing afraid of him. *I love you*, he would murmur. *If only you knew how much.* He'd grip her painfully at the shoulders, his mouth tight on hers, his body hurting her. In museums and galleries he quietly mocked her opinions. "You don't know anything about art," he would say, scornfully shaking his head, if she liked something by someone who wasn't Rembrandt, someone he felt competitive with, someone his own age, someone who was a woman.

She began going alone, as now, whizzing around the gallery partitions and then stopping, long, in front of a piece she liked, one that pulled her in and danced a little before letting her go. She liked scenes, something with water and a boat, but she rarely found any. Mostly there was only what she called Warning Label art: *Like Man*, said one. *Love Hates*, said another.

Or she would go to a movie. A boy with a plate in his head falls in love with a girl who spurns him. He kidnaps her, feeds her, then kills her by opening up her skull to put a plate in there, too. He props her up in a chair and paints watercolors of her in the nude.

On the subway back, in the afternoon, every beggar seemed to her to have Rudy's face, turning, leering. They would come upon her suddenly, sit next to her and belch, take out a harmonica and play an old folk tune. Or sit far away and just look. She would glance up, and every bum in the car would have his stare, persistent as pain.

She got off at Fourth Avenue and dropped her jar off at the clinic.

"We'll telemail you the results," said a young man in a silvery suit, a technician who eyed her warily.

"All right," she said.

To console herself she went to a shop around the corner and tried on clothes. She and Rudy used to do this sometimes, two young poor people, posing in expensive outfits, just to show the other what they would look like *if only*. They would step out of the dressing rooms and curtsy and bow, exasperating the salesperson. Then they would return all the clothes to the racks, go home, make love. Once, before he left the store, Rudy pulled a formal suit off the rack and screamed, "I don't go to these places!" That same night, in the throes of a nightmare, he had groped for the hatchet beneath him and raised it above her, his mouth open, his eyes gone. "Wake up," she'd pleaded, and squeezed his arm until he lowered it, staring emptily at her, confusion smashed against recognition, a surface broken for air.

"COME HERE," Rudy said, when she got home. He had made a dinner of fruit and spinach salad, plus large turkey drumsticks that had been on sale—a Caveman Special. He was a little drunk. The painting he had been working on, Mamie could see now, was of a snarling dog *leaping upon* a Virgin Mary, tearing at her lederhosen—not a good sign. Next to the canvas, cockroaches were smashed on the floor like maple creams.

"I'm tired, Rudy," she said.

"Come on." The cabbagey rot of his one bad molar drifted toward her like a cloud. She moved away from him. "After dinner I want you to go for a walk with me, then. At least." He belched.

"All right." She sat down at the table and he joined her. The television was on, a rerun of *Lust for Life*, Rudy's favorite movie.

"What a madman, Van Gogh," he drawled. "Shooting himself in the stomach. Any sane person would shoot themselves in the head."

"Of course," said Mamie, staring into the spinach leaves; orange sections lay dead on the top like goldfish. She chewed on the turkey leg, which was gamy and dry. "This is delicious, Rudy." *Any sane person would shoot themselves in the head.* For dessert there was a candy bar, split in two.

They went out. It was dusk, the sun not setting as quickly as in January, when it descended fast as a window shade, but now slowing a little, a lingering, hesitant light. A black eye yellowing. They walked together down the slope toward South Brooklyn, into the streak of orange that would soon be night. They seemed somehow to be racing one another, first one of them slightly ahead, then the other. They passed the old brick row homes, the St. Thomas Aquinas Church, the station stop for the F train and the G, that train that went nowhere, it was said, because it went from Brooklyn to Queens, never to Manhattan; no one was ever on it.

They continued walking beneath the el. A train roared deafeningly above them. The streetlights grew sparse, the houses smaller, fenced and slightly collapsed, like the residents of an old folks' home, waiting to die and staring. What stores there were were closed and dark. A skinny black Labrador in front of one of them sniffed at some bags of garbage, nuzzled them as if they were dead bodies that required turning to reveal the murder weapon, the ice pick in the back. Rudy took Mamie's hand. Mamie could feel it—hard, scaly, chapped from turpentine, the nails ridged as seashells, the thumbs blackened by accidents on the job, dark blood underneath, growing out. "Look at your hands," said Mamie, stopping and holding his hand under a streetlight. There was melted chocolate still on his palm, and he pulled it away self-consciously, wiped it on his coat. "You should use some lotion or something, Rudy. Your hands are going to fall off and land on the sidewalk with a big clank."

"So don't hold them."

The Gowanus Canal lay ahead of them. Already the cold sour smell of it, milky with chemicals, blew onto their faces. "Where are we going, anyway?" she asked. A man in a buttonless coat approached them from the bridge, then crossed and kept walking. "This is a little weird, isn't it, being out here at this hour?" They had come to the drawbridge over the canal and stopped. It was strange, this toxic little vein, strange to stand above it, looking down at night, in a dangerous neighborhood, as if they were in love and entitled to such adventures. Sometimes it seemed she and Rudy were two people attempting to tango, sweating and trying, long after the orchestra had grown tired, long after everyone else had gone home.

Rudy leaned his arms on the railing of the bridge, and another train roared over them, an F train, with its raspberry-pink square. "This is the highest elevated in the city," he said, though the train was drowning him out.

Once the train had passed, Mamie murmured, "I know." When Rudy started giving tours of Brooklyn like this, she knew something was the matter.

"Don't you bet there are bodies in this water? Ones the papers haven't notified us of yet? Don't you bet that there are mobsters, and molls, and just the bodies of women that men never learned to love?"

"Rudy, what are you saying?"

"I'll bet there are more bodies here," he said, and for a moment Mamie could see the old familiar rage in his face, though it flew off again, like a bird, and in that moment there seemed nothing on his face at all, a station between trains, until his features pitched suddenly inward, and he began to cry into the sleeves of his coat, into his hard, gravelly hands.

"Rudy, what is it?" She stood behind him and held him, put her arms around his waist, her cheek against his back. There had been times he had consoled her this way, times when he had simply rubbed her back and connected her again to something: Those times when it seemed she'd floated off and was living far away, he had been like a medium calling her from the dead. "Here we are in the Backrub Cave," he'd said, hovering above her, the quilt spread over them both in a small, warm hut, all the ages of childhood returning to her with his hands. Life was long enough so that you could keep relearning things, think and feel and realize again what you used to know.

He coughed and didn't turn around. "I want to prove to my parents I'm not a fuck-up." Once, when he was twelve, his father had offered to drive him to Andrew Wyeth's house. "You wanna be an artist, dontcha, son? Well, I found out where he lives!"

"It's a little late to be worrying about what our parents think of us," she said. Rudy tended to cling to things that were beside the point—the point was always too frightening. Another train roared by, and the water beneath them wafted up sour and sulfuric. "What is it, really, Rudy? What is it you fear?"

"The Three Stooges," he said. "Poverty, Obscurity, Masturbation. Also the three E's. Ennui. Anomie. Misery. Give me one good reason why we should go on living." He was shouting.

"Sorry," she sighed. She pulled away from him, brushed

something from his coat. "You've caught me on a bad day." She searched his profile for an emotion, one that had found dress but not weapons. "I mean, it's life or nothing, right? You don't have to love it, you only have to—" She couldn't think of what.

"We live in a terrible world," he said, and he turned to look at her, wistful and in pain. She could smell that acrid, animal smell hot under his arms. He could smell like that sometimes, like a crazy person. One time she mentioned it, and he went immediately to perfume himself with her bath powder, coming to bed smelling like her. Another time, mistaking the container, he sprinkled himself all over with Ajax.

"Happy Valentine's Day."

"Yes," she said, fear thick in her voice. "Can we go back now?"

*He would sit among them with great dignity and courtesy. "You must pray to this god of yours that keeps you so well. You must pray to him to let us live. Or, if we are to die, let us then go live with your god so that we too may know him." There was silence among the Englishmen. "You see," added the chief, "we pray to our god, but he does not listen. We have done something to offend." Then the chief would stand, go home, remove his English clothes, and die* (picture).

GOZ WAS IN the ladies' room again, and she smiled as Mamie entered. "Going to ask me about my love life?" she said, flossing her teeth in front of the mirror. "You always do."

"All right," said Mamie. "How's your love life?"

Goz sawed back and forth with the floss, then tugged it out. "I don't have a love life. I have a *like* life."

Mamie smiled. She thought how nice that might be, to be peacefully free from love—love and its desire for itself—a husband and wife like two army buddies with stories and World Series bets.

"It's pure, it's stripped, it's friendly. Coffee and dispassion. You should try it." She ducked into one of the stalls and locked it. "Nothing is safe anymore," she called out from inside.

MAMIE LEFT, went to a record store, and bought records. No one had been buying them for years now, and you could get them for seventy-five cents. She bought only albums that had a song with the word *heart* in the title: *The Vernacular Heart, Hectic Heart, A Heart Is Just a Bicycle Behind Your Ribs*. Then she had to leave. Outside the dizzying heat of the store, she clutched them to her chest and walked, down through the decaying restaurant smells of Chinatown toward the Brooklyn Bridge. The sidewalks were fetid and wet, and the day was warm, as if spring had already come. Everyone was out walking. She would stop at the clinic on the way home and drop off her jar.

She thought of a dream she had had the night before. In the dream a door in the apartment opened up and suddenly there were more rooms, rooms she hadn't known existed, a whole house beneath, which was hers. There were birds living inside, and everything was very dark but beautiful, room after room, with windows open for the birds. On the walls were needlepoint samplers that read: *Die Here*. The real estate agent with the scarf kept saying, "In this day and age" and "It's a steal." Goz was there, her blond hair tipped in red and growing dark roots. Tricolor like candy corn. "Just us girls," she kept saying. It was the end of the world, and they were supposed to live there together, as long as it took to die, until their gums felt strange and they got colds and lost their hair, the television all dots and snow. She remembered some sort of movement—bunched and panicky, through stairwells, corridors, dark tunnels hidden behind paintings—and then, in the dream, it untangled to a fluttering stasis.

When she reached the bridge, she noticed some commotion, a disturbance up ahead, halfway across. Two helicopters were circling in the sky, and there was a small crowd at the center of the pedestrian walk. A fire truck and a police car whizzed by beneath her on the right, lights flashing. She walked to the edge of the crowd. "What is it?" she asked a man.

"Look." He pointed toward another man, who had climbed out over the iron mesh and crossbeams, out to the far railing of the bridge. His wrists were banded in black, and his hands held on to the suspension cables. His back arched and his body swayed out over the water below, as if caught in a web of steel parallelograms. His head dangled like someone crucified, and the wind tore through his hair. In the obscured profile, she thought she could make out the features.

"Oh, my God," she said.

"The woman in front of us says he's the guy wanted for the Gowanus Canal murders. See the police boats circling down there?" Two red-and-white speedboats were churning up water. One of the helicopters hovered noisily above.

"Oh, my God," Mamie said again, and pushed her way through the crowd. A white heat burst in her brain. A police motorbike pulled up on the walkway behind her. A policeman with pistols got off. "It's someone I know," Mamie repeated to people, and elbowed them aside. "It's someone I know." She held her purse and bag in front of her and pushed. The policeman was following close behind, so she pressed hard. When she came to the place directly across from the man, she put down her things and lifted her knee up onto the rail, swung her leg over, and began to crawl, metal to skin, toward the outer reaches of the bridge. "Hey!" someone shouted. The policeman. "Hey!" Cars sped beneath her, and an oceany wind rushed into her mouth. She tried not to look down. "Rudy!" she called out, but it seemed feeble in the roar, her throat a half throat. "It's me!" She felt surrounded by sky, moving toward it, getting closer. Her nails broke against metal. She *was* getting closer, close enough, soon, to grab him, to talk to him, to take his face in her hands and say something about *let's go home*. But then suddenly, too far from her, he relinquished his grip on the cables and fell, turning, his limbs like a windmill, vanishing into the East River below.

She froze. *Rudy*. Two people screamed. There was a whirring noise from the crowd behind her, people pressed to the railings. *No, not this*. "Excuse me, m'am," shouted a voice. "Did you say you knew this man?"

She inched backward on her knees, lowered herself to the walkway. Her legs were scraped and bleeding, but she didn't feel them. Someone was touching her, clamping hands around her arms. Her purse and bag were still where she'd left them, leaning against the cement, and she jerked free, grabbed them, and began to run.

She ran the rest of the way across the bridge, down into the ammonia dank of a passageway, then up again to an old ruined park, zigzagging through the fruit streets of the Heights— Cranberry, Pineapple—along the hexagonal cobbles of the promenade, along the water, and then up left, in a ricochet against the DON'T WALK lights. She did not stop running even when she found herself in Carroll Gardens, heading toward the Gowanus Canal. *No, not this*. She ran up the slope of South Brooklyn for twenty minutes, through traffic, through red lights and sirens, beneath the scary whoop of helicopters and a bellowing plane, until she reached the house with the bird feeder, and when she got there, scarcely able to breathe, she sank down on the concrete lip of its fence and let out a cry, solitary and strangled, into her bag of songs.

THE AFTERNOON DARKENED. Two Rosies shuffled by, ignoring her, but slowing down, winded. They, too, decided to sit on the low wall of the fence, but chose to do so at some distance. She had already slid into the underclass of the sick, she knew, but they didn't recognize her yet. "Are you OK?"

she heard one Rosie say to the other, putting her box of flowers down on the sidewalk.

"I'm OK," said her friend.

"You look worse."

"Maybe," she sighed. "The thing is you never know why you're any particular place. You get up, you move. You keep thinking there's some other way than this."

"Look at *her*," snorted the friend, motioning toward Mamie.

"What?" said the other, and then they fell silent.

A fire truck clanged by. Sirens wailed in outrage. After some time Mamie got up, slow as an arthritic, clutching only her purse—her jar still in it—leaving the records behind. She began to walk, stumbling on a raised crack in the pavement. And she noticed something: The house with the bird feeder didn't have a cupola at all. It didn't even have a bird feeder. It simply had a sign that said RESTAURANT, and there was a pigeon on it.

She walked by the Rosies and gave them a dollar for an iris. "My," said the one handing it to her.

At the apartment, the lights were on and the padlock hung open like a hook. She stood for a moment, then kicked at the door with her foot, banging the inside knob against the wall. There was no other sound, and she hesitated there in the doorway, a form of desire, a hovering thing that cannot enter a room. But slowly she took a step, the heel of her hand pressed to the doorjamb to steady her.

He was there, hair dry, wearing different clothes. His arms were raised over his head, the stray tom like a mast in his hands on top. He was moving slowly around the place, as if in a deep Oriental exercise or a dance, the cat investigating the bookshelves.

"It's you," Mamie said, frozen by the open door.

The pumpkin stench of the bathroom wafted toward her. The uriney cold rushed in from behind, carrying with it the flap of helicopters. He turned to see her, brought the cat down to his chest. "Hi." He was chewing on a difficult bit of candy, pieces of it stuck in his teeth. He pointed to his cheek, grimacing. "Jujubes," he said. "They play with your mind."

The television burst on: people chanting together, like an anthem for cola. *We are the Undying. We are . . .*

He turned away and lifted the cat up high again, close to the golden moldings of the ceiling. "Cats love this," he said. His arms were long and tireless. In the reach, his shirt had come untucked, and the soft bare skin of his waist flashed like a smile. "Where have you been?"

There was only this world, this looted, ventriloquized earth. If one were to look for a place to die, mightn't it be here?—like some old lesson of knowing your kind and returning. She was afraid, and the afraid, she realized, sought opportunities for bravery in love. She tucked the flower in her blouse. Life or death. Something or nothing. *You want something or nothing?*

She stepped toward him with a heart she'd someday tear the terror from.

Here. But not now.

A NOTE ON THE TYPE

*The text of this book was set in a digitized version of a typeface known as Garamond. The design is based on letter forms originally created by Claude Garamond (c. 1480–1561). Garamond was a pupil of Geoffroy Tory and may have patterned his letter forms on Venetian models. To this day, the typeface that bears his name is one of the most attractive used in book composition, and the intervening years have caused it to lose little of its freshness or beauty.*

*Composed by PennSet, Inc.,*
*Bloomsburg, Pennsylvania*
*Printed and bound by Fairfield Graphics,*
*Fairfield, Pennsylvania*
*Typography and binding design by*
*Iris Weinstein*